THE EINSTEIN GIRL

Philip Sington was born in Cambridge. His father was an industrial chemist and his mother an officer in British Intelligence. After studying History at Trinity College, Cambridge he worked as a business journalist and magazine editor for nine years. He co-authored six novels under the joint pseudonym Patrick Lynch, selling well over a million copies worldwide. His first solo novel, *Zoia's Gold*, was published in 2005. To date his work has been translated into eighteen foreign languages. He lives in London with his family.

1.

The body lay face up with that crumpled, unsymmetrical look of death. Its arms were tossed in careless surrender. One leg was twisted under the other in the shape of a 4. The coat, too, was flung wide, showing the bloody shirt that had dried to a wad of dark stain. The trouser pockets, inside out, hung lifeless. Homicide detective Gabriel Wager, Denver Police Department, bent carefully over the sprawled figure and, with a gentle tug, slipped a neatly folded piece of paper from the stiff fingers.

"It's sure as hell no suicide note." Max Axton, Wager's partner, loomed over his shoulder as Wager used the eraser end of a pencil to unfold the page carefully. As Max said, "A man with his chest punched open like that wouldn't turn his own pockets inside out while he died."

"Hold the bag open."

Axton spread the plastic bag with his fingers and Wager slipped the paper in. He pressed shut the ridge that sealed it, and labeled the item with the date, his initials, and the location.

"What is it, some kind of sketch?"

"It looks like a butterfly," Wager said.

Max peered more closely. "Naw—it's an angel. The wings are curved at the top. And that's the robe." He pressed the corners of the plastic bag to stretch away the wrinkles. "It's holding something."

"A sword," Wager said. "It's an angel holding a sword."

Axton nodded and frowned with thought. "I don't know any gangs with that symbol. Does it ring a bell with you?"

"No." Wager gazed at the paper with its measured creases and the darkly inked lines of the figure. It wasn't crumpled or dirty; if a dying man had clutched at it the scrap of paper would have been wrinkled.

"I'll take the witness," said Axton.

"Okay." Behind him, Wager heard the slowing rush of motors as drivers paused to gawk at the line of a half-dozen patrol units and unmarked cars tilted on the road's shoulder, and at the blue uniforms moving slowly over the corner of weed-choked prairie. When they were past the row of cars, the motors sped up again, pulling the drivers home from haze-shrouded Denver toward the dozens of suburban developments spreading eastward across the plains.

"You guys believe me, don't you?"

Wager looked at the witness. The bearded young man was suddenly nervous, and beneath his shaggy hair worry pinched his brows.

"Any reason we shouldn't?"

"No! But . . . I mean . . . all these questions. . . . Honest to God, Officer, I was just hitching along here!"

Axton nodded and shifted his weight from one large shoe to the other. "We understand that, Mr. Garfield. We just want to get everything down now so we don't have to call you up later."

Garfield sucked in a breath and scratched somewhere up under the blond-streaked beard. "Yeah. It's just all of a sudden I thought, Jesus, what if you guys think I did it?"

"We don't know who did it," Wager said. "Yet."

"Can you show me exactly where you were when you first saw the victim, Mr. Garfield?"

Wager left Max with the witness and went back to the body.

Jones, the police photographer, was framing the scene from yet another angle. The thin black man took three or four more shots and then capped his lens. "That's it for the meat, Gabe. What else you want?"

"Get a couple from the witness—where he first saw the body. And one more of the site after the body's been removed."

"Sure thing."

Two ambulance attendants who sat on their stretcher at the shoulder of the road watched in silence. Finally Wager motioned to them. "You people come around this way and take it out the same way."

"We'll need some help up this bank," said the shorter one.

"You'll get it."

Photographs, forensics, field work. But no immediate witnesses. Wager would be surprised if any of it told them much at all. The note was supposed to do that. Without that little drawing of the angel, this would look like only one more of the casual stranger-to-stranger murders that were becoming routine in booming, shoving Denver—the tossing away of a human being for a watch, a ring, a few bucks. But for some reason this killer left his signature. For some reason he wanted somebody to know something about this death. An execution? An advertisement? A dope deal gone wrong? Forensics would find out if the victim was a user.

The ambulance attendants, lips tight as though trying to pinch out a bad taste, strained slightly to break the rigor in the corpse's shoulder joints. The body would not fit through the ambulance doors with the arms spread like that, and they had to strap them, bent at the elbows, across the chest to keep them from lifting open again. The rigor told Wager that the man was probably shot right here. Probably the killer or killers walked the victim straight down the embankment and stood just there while he turned to face them. Wind. Almost always a night wind out here on the prairie east of Denver and its bright glow. Maybe a step or two closer for a good shot. Maybe early this morning before dawn, where the lights of the few passing cars would not splash across the man or the gun aimed at him. Perhaps the victim's arms were already held out—don't shoot me, I don't have anything; perhaps they flew up as the bullet hit his chest like a baseball bat and knocked him flat and numb with shock and dead before he hit the ground. A hole that close to the heart and that big. Soon enough, anyway, so he did not move before he died and stiffened in that awkward angle. The killer may have waited, may even have moved close to look at the victim, to make sure a second round from that heavy-caliber weapon was not needed. Then he—or they—went through the pockets very quickly, not needing a light because of the sky glow of Denver. Careful of fingerprints, hurriedly gathering keys, coins, matches—anything the killer's fingers might touch while going through the pockets for whatever he was after. Then that note, which was to tell someone why the man was shot, if not who pulled the trigger. Wager guessed that the note had been folded and resting in the killer's pocket, ready for use. Folded precisely into a rectangle whose edges were flush all around. When you're in the dark, and in a hurry, and you've just killed a man, you don't take time to align the edges of a folded slip of paper. That's something you do when you're carefully planning ahead. Then you put it where you know you can find it, so that when you're sure the fingers have stopped living you can wedge it high up between them so it won't blow away. Then back up the way you came, through those broken weeds and the matted earth that left no footprints in the bricklike clay. And, probably, you stepped into your car to pull onto the empty highway, mingling your tire prints with the dozens of tracks that Baird was busy casting in plaster of Paris.

"Detective Wager?" One of the uniformed officers picked his way through the tangles of Russian thistles. "We been all over the grid twice—didn't find a thing." He watched the ambulance attendants and two policemen scrabble the heavy stretcher up the embankment.

Wager nodded. The fact that nothing had been found outside the ten-foot radius fit the feeling he had about this killing: it was a quick and efficient assassination. And by this time, the killer could have run anywhere.

"You gonna want us for anything else? The shift's due off in a few minutes."

"No—send your people back. Thanks, Clark." No sense wasting the overtime; the city council already screamed at the cost of police work at the same time that it screamed about the rising homicide rate.

"You and Max stop by for coffee next time you're in the district."

"Thanks."

Only half aware of the retreating sergeant, Wager let his mind play over the scene again, trying to see it from the angle of the victim. Then from that of the killer. Night. Over there, beyond the straggling line of officers working their way back toward the cars, a few distant lights from one of the newer housing developments. A car or two heard in the distance, passing across the dim haze of city lights. That's what the victim would have seen: the glare of Denver's lights against the sky, and in front of that the killer's black shape. A fraction of an instant before it hit him, he may have seen the belch of flame start to spread toward him. He would not have felt the heat. The bullet would have been in front of the heat. The killer would have moved a step or two closer, with maybe a pause to check for movement. Then pulled the pockets inside out, taking everything—no empty wallet flung aside, no half-used package of cigarettes or gum, or comb with the stray hair snarled in its teeth. The killer wanted time to look over everything found in those pockets. Something in those pockets would say things the killer knew the victim would not tell him while he was alive. Then he placed the square of paper.

Finally Wager walked up toward Baird, who was now standing to stretch his sore back as he watched the plaster harden in its frame.

"I got Garfield's statement, Gabe. Clark says one of his people can give him a ride over to I-225."

"That's where the kid was going?"

"Yeah. He lives out in Aurora." Axton folded his notebook closed with a hand that almost hid the small book. They watched Jones come back to the spot of flattened weeds and lean over the stained earth to flash the Speed Graphic. Jones pulled the film slide and jotted down the number and time and location of the picture.

"Tomorrow morning soon enough for these?"

"Sure."

"Ciao."

"Did Baird find any footprints?" asked Max.

Wager shook his head. "The ground's too hard." He rummaged in the small kit for the tape measure and a handful of flat cardboard boxes. "Let's do it while we've got the light."

"Right," said Axton.

Together, they began to pick over the area around the

stained earth. They stepped carefully through tangled grass and bent to peer for the occasional scrap of paper or cigarette butt. They picked up the item with tweezers and put it in one of the boxes, then taped the box shut and labeled it with their initials and the distance and direction from the stain. It was garbage. It would be screened in the lab for weathering and age and potential usefulness, but Wager guessed that all of it would be tossed out as useless, because this murderer had come here knowing what he was going to do, and he had been careful when he did it.

But there was always the chance. That's what following procedure meant: you used routine like a net to sift for those stray chances. So they would search and pick and label until there was nothing left in that three hundred square feet except the earth and weeds and the stain.

After a while, Axton and Wager traded ground, moving back over the sectors from the opposite direction like, it crossed Wager's mind, a pair of well-trained hounds ranging for spoor. Wager's triangular shadow, disproportionately wide at the shoulders and tapering quickly to his feet, lengthened to absorb the crisp lines from twigs and stems; Axton's broad shadow stretched beyond Wager's in a patient, slow ripple. Neither man found anything the other had overlooked; neither said more than was necessary. But of course that wasn't from concentration alone. That was because almost a year ago Wager had set up a scumbag called Tony-O. At the time Axton had called it lynch law and said it was the wrong thing for a cop to do and tried to talk Wager out of it. But Wager knew then and knew now that the execution was just. Not legal, maybe, but just; and he'd be damned if he'd apologize to Max or anyone else for doing that to a man who had violated more than the criminal code.

"Satisfied?"

"Yeah," said Wager.

They scraped off a sample of topsoil into a plastic bag and labeled that; then they packed the kit and trudged up the bank toward their car, the only one remaining this late after quitting time. As a final effort, they followed the likely path of the killer, but nothing more was found there either.

"How many John Does we had this year?" sighed Axton.

"Seventeen." Of which thirteen had been cleared because someone had eventually identified the victim, traced his last movements, and, with a lot of walking and talking, finally found someone who remembered something. Something that led to a suspect. "But none of them plastered with angels."

"Right," sighed Axton again. "Our first angel."

He grunted slightly while wedging himself behind the steering wheel. The department had gone to smaller-sized cars, and even with the seat jammed against the backstops, Axton's frame was cramped. Wager rolled the window down to let in the peppery air of evening, its lingering heat blowing dry and not yet refreshing across his ear.

"Gabe—ah—you got any plans for the fifteenth of next month?"

"The fifteenth? That's a long way off. What's the fifteenth?"

"It's a Saturday." Axton kept his attention focused on the driving. "Polly's planning a little get-together. A barbecue."

Wager glanced at Max. His profile looked as jagged as the mountain range silhouetted behind him: heavy brow jutting over the notch at the bridge of his nose, that nose rippling out across its break and then sharply back to the full mouth, then the long curve of a chin that came out farther than the nose and swung down and back to a size-nineteen neck. Wager enjoyed watching a suspect's eyes when they first saw Max crowd into an interview cubicle. They always went first to the face, then, as they measured the torso and realized his size, they went guardedly back to that craggy nose. Occasionally, Wager smiled and introduced him to the suspect: "This is Detective Axton. Some people call him Max-the-Ax."

"I might have a date with Jo," said Wager. "It depends on the duty roster."

"She'll be welcome, too. It's nothing formal," Axton added quickly. "Just a cookout for whoever shows up, and you and Jo are welcome."

A casual barbecue planned that far in advance. That was like Polly: arranging her world and everyone else's, and using Axton's easygoing ways as her reason for being so organized. And it was like Axton to pretend that the invitation was nothing special. Wager watched the eastern horizon shade into darker and darker purple, the way night comes across the prairie through dusty summer air. There was nothing to catch the low-lying sun except the wavering ranks of new suburban rooftops, and they, too, rolled steadily under into dusk. "Polly's not mad at me anymore?"

"Aw, come on, Gabe! As soon as she found out what the problem was, she understood. I get that way, too—we all do; she understands it's the job. It's just that she knows my signals and she didn't know yours."

"Your 'signals'? You and Golding been talking body language again?"

"Did I say that?" Axton's head wagged. "Well, there may be some truth in it."

No truth that anyone with a pair of eyes and half a brain hadn't already figured out by the time he was ten years old. But that excluded Golding. "He hasn't said much about acupuncture lately. He give up on that?"

"I think so. He had a book—*Acupuncture as a Hobby*—but he couldn't find anybody to practice on. Except himself, and I guess that didn't work out too well."

"Maybe we should use him in interrogation."

Max's eyes slanted in Wager's direction as if he wasn't quite certain whether or not he was joking. "Anyway, the invitation's there. Polly wanted me to tell you."

Body language or no body language, it had taken Polly long enough to understand why her carefully planned evening had been spoiled by his fight with Axton about Tony-O. But Wager said nothing about that because they weren't really talking about Polly or her dinner. This was something more important—it was about Max, his partner. And the reason for that fight and the coolness that resulted. It was the first time since the Tony-O thing that Axton had said a word about getting together outside a patrol car.

But if it took Axton almost a year to get over blaming him for something he knew was damn well right, then maybe Wager wasn't too eager to kiss and make up.

"That's a long way off," he said again.

"I hope you can make it." Axton's eyes were back studying the light traffic of the freeway. "I mean that."

And, just maybe, Wager had his own pride, which Axton had stepped on. "I'll check with Jo."

The rest of the ride was in the silence that had become habitual and almost without strain during the past months: two people arbitrarily yoked together to put in their time. Neither one had been willing to go to Chief Doyle to ask for a change of partner because that would have been acting like a prima donna. Golding might have done it, but not Wager or Axton. Homicide was a small division, and there wasn't room to coddle personalities. Especially if neither man could tell the division chief the real reason for such a request. But if Axton felt guilty because his partner had abetted a homicide, that was his problem. Wager felt no guilt at all. He was, as he'd heard people call him, a tough little spic bastard, and he was proud of it. What the hell, you didn't have to like your partner; all you had to do was work with him. Wager could tell himself that, and he could almost believe it.

When he reached his shadowy apartment, the little light on Wager's telephone-answering machine glowed red for Message Received. Reading the instruction booklet once more, he carefully pressed the Rewind button and waited as the tape whirred dryly. The machine was new, a toy really, and though he wouldn't be shy about admitting he owned one, neither did Wager tell the world about it. For one thing, he was still suspicious of the home-gadget industry and the fact that Golding had bought one and praised it for three weeks straight. For another, it was nobody's business what Wager did with his money. And he'd bought the machine for good reason: there were occasions when people wanted to talk to him without having to go through a police switchboard. Usually those voices came on the tape with a hurried "Wager, it's me—I got something for you. Get in touch with me quick, will you?"

But this wasn't an informant. The Play button brought the slightly nasal voice of a policewoman in Missing Persons, responding to the note he had left there before he went home for the day.

"Detective Wager, we have no report of a missing person matching that John Doe description you gave us. We should have a report from the national listing sometime tomorrow."

The tape clicked and then ran long enough to tell him that was the only message. He pressed Rewind and Off and dialed the police laboratory. A recording of Baird's voice told him what he already knew: the laboratory was closed and would be open tomorrow morning at eight. Please call back. *Click.*

Wager hung up and gazed through the glass doors to his balcony at the scarlet feathers of cloud hanging beyond the ragged lines of mountains. At this altitude, the summer light lasted well into evening, and there were times, like now, when the sun touched wisps of cloud lingering a hundred miles away across the Rockies. If he were in those mountains, say camped beside one of those small lakes that looked as if they clung to the earth's tilted flanks, this would be the time for those last few casts. The mosquitoes and night insects would be out, the still water circled here and there with rising trout and the quick touch of dipping insects. Just the time for half a dozen quiet casts; time to try for that last savage strike and the intense play of taut line against the surge and leap of the fish out of the placid mirror.

But he was here, ten stories above a downtown Denver street that echoed with the urgent summer noises of automobiles and the shuffle and scrape of feet made restless by the warm night. There was a different kind of fishing down here; perhaps a different kind of savagery. Wager wasn't so certain about that, though; muggers, rapists, killers—they struck, like any other animal, at the weak, the crippled, the defenseless. They came out of dark crevices between buildings and went after the sure thing as a fish lunged after a wobbling minnow. Except for executioners. Executioners were different.

An angel holding a sword. Michael, the sword of the Lord, prince of celestial armies. That was the picture Wager remembered from one of the stained-glass windows when he had fidgeted through another of Father Shannon's droning sermons in old San Cajetano's. Michael

holding his sword before him while below his left foot
Adam and Eve slunk away—the top half of Adam, anyway.
Eve's blond head peeked over his shoulder, and the teenage Wager had only been able to imagine faintly what the
rest of her looked like. Below Michael's right foot, a ser-
pentine Satan recoiled in fear, and Father Shannon would
point to that glowing scene in every sermon against fleshly
lust.

Father Shannon: a grim man, more like a Lutheran than
a Catholic. "He doesn't have a warm soul," his mother
used to murmur in Spanish. "He doesn't have the soul of
a man who serves God with love." And his father, whose
Spanish, like his adopted faith, often stumbled, would grin.
"Maybe he serves God with fear. He sure as hell scares me
sometimes!" Michael was gonna get you if you didn't
watch out.

Wager reported before eight the next morning. Munn,
who was getting an ulcer worrying about his ulcer coming
back, was glad to check out a half hour early.

"I'll be goddamn happy to get off this shift." The baggy-
eyed detective leaned for a moment against the metal
door frame of the homicide unit's suite of partitioned
offices and sculpted plastic furniture. The department had
finally moved into the new Justice Center, but Wager had
not yet gotten used to the expanse of space that surrounded each desk, and his elbows and knees were still
cautious. "There's nobody to talk to," said Munn. "I got too
much time to think."

"What do you think about?"

"My ulcer. I can feel the sonofabitch. I can feel it start
to grow."

"Take some sick leave, Munn."

"I used it all. I just hope I can hang on until retirement." A sour look crossed his face as his mind turned to something inside. "I got to go. Thanks, Gabe." He went hurriedly toward the men's room down the hushed and carpeted hall.

Wager punched the telephone number for the laboratory. The recording started and then with an abrupt squeak broke into Baird's real voice. "Lab. Sergeant Baird."

"This is Gabe, Fred. What do you have on that victim we found yesterday?"

"Right now, Wager, I got a cup of coffee sitting on his file. The working day hasn't started yet."

A cop's working day never stopped, not unless he got transferred to a desk somewhere away from the street and away from a world that never stopped either. But when that happened, you weren't a real cop anymore. "I could use an i.d. on him, Baird. There's not much we can do until we know who he is."

"Gabe, I really am working on him. I'm filling out the background forms right now, and I'll be going to the morgue in about five minutes. You can even come with me and watch if you want."

"I'll be right there."

He left a note telling Axton where to find him, and after a few twists and turns through the color-coordinated hallways he cleared the security door to the new laboratory. The brochure printed by the department for the taxpayers who toured the recently built Justice Center said it was the most complete and modern forensics laboratory outside the FBI lab back at Washington. What the brochure did not say was that the department budget had not yet authorized any more people; most of the new equipment and space was still unused. Call it planning ahead: in another twenty years, the Denver area was supposed to double in size because of Colorado's energy boom. Then the lab would be too small.

Baird was at his desk along one of the walls that caught light from the tinted and sealed windows high above the street. Somewhere behind the tangle of glass piping and chrome stands a Bunsen burner gave its soft hiss and an unseen hand clinked a stirring rod. Baird glanced up when he heard Wager's shoes on the tile floor. "There's the report on the clothing—I got that done last night. Working overtime. Your copy's on top."

Wager glanced down the slip. "It doesn't say much."

"Don't blame me."

The victim's pockets had yielded lint and dust of a non-definitive nature. The cuffless trousers had a little bit more: a couple of seeds that had not been identified, and a film of dust trapped in the vacuum bag. Both were on their way by registered mail to the FBI for classification. The shoes, too, had been delicately cleaned and the scrapings of each packaged and forwarded. The label from inside the coat was from a men's store in Salt Lake City, Utah; no other identifying labels or laundry marks had been found.

"How long—"

"Possibly twelve to twenty-four hours." Baird, thinning hair showing his pink crown, did not look up as he finished the form with signature and date. "The coroner will pin it down better. Let's go."

The basement of Denver General Hospital served as the morgue for DPD. Wager drove, then followed as Baird, lugging his metal case, stenciled DPD LAB—FINGERPRINT, walked through the tiled and echoing halls to the cool room with its bank of drawers like a gigantic filing cabinet. A young orderly who looked slightly hung over rolled out the drawer. A puff of cold, artificially scented air came with it. "Give me a call when you're finished."

"Right."

Baird pulled off the coarse sheet. The body, its torn chest black from the blood dried beneath the bruised skin and mottled with lividity marks on buttocks and shoulders, stared with half-open eyes at the fluorescent panels of the ceiling. In the field, Wager seldom looked closely at a victim's face—a glance, maybe, for identification, then he focused on the wound and the body in general and especially on the site. It made the corpse seem less human, less a perversion of the everyday world. But here in the antiseptic glare of the morgue, the humanness was washed away and he could study the face as if it were an object under glass. Now he saw the victim more clearly than he had when it lay in the field. In this flat light he could see that the gray-streaked hair had receded far up the man's curving forehead; at the side of his neck, like hashmarks leading up to the hairy earlobes, sharp wrinkles creased the dry skin. The prominent nose and eyebrows marked a narrow face that was already losing its strong characteristics. The gaping lips, which had never been full, now looked like a razor slash through the gray flesh. Wager made a few notes in his little green book.

"You find any needle tracks?"

"No. But the doc'll have to look at the organs to know for sure if he was a user."

"You figure he's around fifty?"

Baird looked up from rummaging in the shelves of his open kit and squinted at the face. "Yeah—he looks like it. We'll try to pin it down a little closer for you."

He laid out his equipment on a wheeled table and began to fold a pair of disposable rubber gloves over his fingers. "I'm not sure how long this is going to take, Wager. There's bound to be some decay already set in. A whole day lying in that sun . . ."

The statement called for no reply. Wager watched as

Baird cupped a crooked forefinger in his hand and pressed with his thumb on the victim's knuckle; the flesh under Baird's thumbnail whitened and after a moment he grunted with pent breath. "Have to use the knife."

"Does the rigidity give you a better idea what time he was killed?"

"A little. But lividity, digestion, ocular fluid—all those things have to be figured in, and the pathologist will get to them. One thing at a time, okay? You were crapping your pants to get fingerprints; fingerprints you're gonna get."

Baird always got prissy when he defended the technicalities of his work. Wager shut up and watched. The lab man's scalpel sliced deeply under the second joint of the fingers and between thumb and forefinger. "Might as well do both hands while the knife's dirty, right?" A paper towel soaked up the seepage. Baird levered each finger straight with a quick motion, as if punching open a can. Then he began gently washing the fingers with soap and water. He used a small toothbrush to lightly work any foreign matter out of the ridges of the fingers and then dribbled a solution on a cotton swab and dabbed at the fingertips. The wet cotton tip followed the swirls and ridges of gray flesh. "Xylene," he said. "Cleans away any oils or grease that soap and water miss." Bending over the awkwardly stiff arms, he rinsed and dried each finger. "All right, now we can go to work."

He picked up a tool like a long, shallow spoon and threaded a strip of fingerprint paper through the notched end. "We'll try the easy way first." He rolled ink on a spatula and pressed that around the bulb of the forefinger; then he slipped the spoon beneath the carefully lifted digit and pressed it firmly down. Raising it carefully again, he drew out the fingerprint and bent over the flattened paper with a magnifying glass.

"Well?"

"Take a look."

Wager did. In the lens, the print of black swirls and ridges had numerous gaps and empty patches, as though someone had half erased the man's fingertips. "Will this be good enough?"

Baird was already filling a syringe from one of the kit's bottles. "No. The fingers have dried out too much—dry climate, hot sun. We'll do a little tissue builder." He jabbed the needle into the underside of the first joint and down beneath the ball of the fingertip. "This is good stuff. Glycerine and water's okay, but they leak out after a while. This stuff sets up. Undertakers use it to fill out sunken tissue." His hands busy, he nodded toward the victim's face. "Like around his eyes. You see where it's already sunk in?"

"I see."

"Expensive, though." He finished and tied a wide thread around each finger below the needle hole. "So the tissue builder won't leak out. It'll be a few minutes." He began rinsing the syringe. "You want some coffee?"

"No." Wager checked the time; he and Axton were supposed to be on the street by now, making rounds. "How long's this going to take?"

"Christ, Wager, it could take all day! If this doesn't work, I try something else. A sodium hydroxide bath, maybe. Sometimes I've had to peel off the fingertips and wrap them around my own. If it's real bad—worse than this one —I have to send both hands to the FBI and they do the work. That may take a week or two before they come back with a good impression. Check with me this afternoon, okay?"

"I'll check at lunch time."

2.

Baird finished his work by noon, but that didn't do Wager much good—the prints cleared both the state and FBI files with no identification; and despite Wager's daily calls, Missing Persons listed no one closely matching the victim's description. After one day, the small article—"Unidentified Man Found Slain"—dropped out of the local news section; after two days, radio and television stopped mentioning the case. By the end of the week, it rested in the "active" drawer, one more thin manila folder with no new information, deserving little attention compared with the steady demands of current stabbings, shootings, bludgeonings. And one garroting, which was sure to make the front page because it broke the routine mayhem.

"Wager, I hate to ask you this—in fact, I hate to ask you anything—but can you give me some reason why a guy would be strangled like that?" Gargan held his reporter's notebook ready. As always, he wore a black turtleneck pullover, a color Wager swore he chose to hide the dirt.

"Maybe somebody didn't like him."

"I knew you were going to say that. I just knew you were

going to say something as corny and predictable as that."

"Then don't ask me anything, Gargan, and we'll both be happier."

The reporter shook his head in disgust. "It's my job to ask, Wager. My goddamn job. And, whether you like it or not, my right, too. The public pays your salary and they've got a right to know just how good, or in your case how lousy, you do your job!" He wandered out of the homicide office in search of anyone else.

A satisfied smile tilted the corners of Wager's mouth as he dialed the number for Vice and Narcotics. The garroting had all the signs of a drug killing, and Politzki over in Johns and Junkies was a good place to start. But Gargan didn't have to find that out from Wager. If the reporter had a right to know, he also had a duty to work for his stories, and over the past years each man had done what he could to make the other's work a little harder.

"Vice and Narcotics, Sergeant Politzki."

"This is Wager in Homicide. I think we've got a victim you might know: Ellison, Michael David."

"Ellison . . . ? Black kid? Around twenty-five?"

"That's him."

"Where'd you dig him up? Ha."

Politzki enjoyed making the kind of jokes he heard on television. And like his favorite television shows, he provided his own laugh track. "Over near the Zuñi power plant. What can you tell me about him?"

"Not much, Wager. He's not heavy—a chipper and a mule, mostly. What'd he do, get ambitious?"

"It looks that way."

"Happens all the time." And if he was dead, he was no longer Vice and Narcotics' worry. He was Wager's. "He's got a jacket. That'll tell you more than I can."

"Thanks, Ski."

"My pleasure, Gabe. I mean that, ha!"

Wager, like Gargan, would have to get his own story. Sighing, he stood and gathered up the homicide report in its secondhand manila folder and went down to Records.

Where Policewoman Josephine Fabrizio smiled as she caught sight of Wager leaning over the wide shelf looking for her.

"Hi." That's all she said, but the smile and the way she sounded told Wager a lot more, and he felt again that surprised sense of warmth and completeness he rediscovered every time they saw each other.

"You are one very sexy cop, Policeperson Fabrizio."

"That sounds more like monkey business than police business, Detective Sergeant Wager."

"Right—we don't want to waste the taxpayers' money. But when you get out of that uniform . . ."

Jo glanced at the clerks busy in front of computer terminals and telephones. "I know what's on your mind—and I love it."

That was the use they gave to the word "love." They loved things about each other, but neither ever said "I love you." They had worn those words thin before they met each other, and, Wager knew, the words still opened doors that neither wanted to explore yet.

"Has the weekend roster been posted?"

She nodded. "I get off at five, Saturday."

"I'll see you at five-oh-one." He told her about the Axtons' invitation. "We don't have to go," he said. "I don't even think I want to."

"Why?"

He shrugged. "Polly worries so damn much about people having a good time that I've never had one there yet."

"Polly invited you? Or Max?"

"Max."

"I thought so. He's trying to patch things up." She added, "He knows you're too stubborn to make the first move."

Wager stifled the angry impulse to say that his partner was his business and his business only. But Jo meant well, and, after all, Wager had let her in on it. During one of those rainy dawns when they lay half asleep and still sweaty and clinging to each other, Wager had described how he had ruined Polly's dinner that time by fighting with his partner. But that was all he told her. If a cop as good as Max could feel guilty about sharing the knowledge of Tony-O's execution, Wager wasn't going to burden Policewoman Fabrizio with it.

"Or didn't you want me to tell you that?" She smiled.

"You don't have to tell me, Querida. All us Hispanos are stubborn. That's how we preserve our colorful heritage against you Anglos."

"Uh-oh—there's that Spanish accent. But don't forget, Pancho, I'm not Anglo. I'm Italiana."

The accent always betrayed his anger. And Jo always seemed to defuse it. He slid his hand across the shelf in mute apology and touched her fingertips. "I'll think about Polly and her damn barbecue. Here, Policeperson Wop, see what you've got on this dude." He showed her the form with Ellison's name.

She glanced down the report. "Strangulation?"

"Low-budget homicide."

"Yuk! It'll take just a minute."

He watched her lean toward the scanner, the taut blue skirt showing the long curve of leg that his hands knew so well. Her dark hair, regulation length and shorter than he liked it on his women, curled to her shoulders and showed the coppery light that some brunettes had. And despite her slimness and the stiff uniform shirt, her breasts showed fully, too. Wager remembered when he first saw her, the chrome name tag, Fabrizio, J., riding above one of those round breasts while a tall blond cop leaned familiarly against her. That guy was gone now, and she never talked of him. Wager never asked.

He shuffled through the Ellison jacket for a list of known associates and the names of various arresting officers who might remember the youth and the people he hung around with. That was where this kind of case usually found its solution, and the tiny whir of the office's electric clock over the entry underscored the routine quality of Wager's work. When the telephone rang he automatically noted the time—twenty to eleven—and pulled a pad of paper to him as he answered. "Homicide, Detective Wager."

But it wasn't another death report; it was Doyle's secretary telling him that the Bulldog wanted to see him as soon as possible. When Wager entered the homicide chief's office, the man's lower teeth in the underslung jaw glinted in a polite way.

The Bulldog motioned Wager to one of the black Leatherette chairs with its embossed seal of the Denver Police Department. Visitors to the offices of division chiefs got to sit on those chairs; molded plastic rested the backsides that visited lesser offices.

"You making any progress on that strangulation case?"

Wager eyed the man. The Ellison case promised to be a garden-variety homicide and not worth Doyle's special notice. "He was a small-time pusher. I'm working on a list of known associates now."

"Keep it legal."

That was Doyle's prejudice against ex-narcs. Wager knew his business. He did not bother to answer.

"What about that John Doe found east of town Monday? Anything?"

He shook his head. "No i.d. yet. Coroner's report, pathology findings. We're still waiting on the dental check. With no i.d., we're not going to get very far."

"Uh-huh." Doyle pushed a leaf of paper across the shiny dark wood of his desk. "Does this look familiar?"

It was the sketch of an angel, domed wings spread and sword upright.

"Another one?"

"It came in the mail this morning. It was found on a victim in Pueblo a couple days ago. Give me everything you've got so far."

Wager told Doyle the findings of the coroner: death by gunshot, an exploding bullet of heavy caliber—probably .44 or .45—sometime in the early morning of the day he was found. No FBI record, no military service, no missing-persons report. The Salt Lake City store that sold the victim's suit did not remember the man's description. No laundry marks.

"Possible motive robbery? Maybe a dope deal?"

"The pathologist found no traces of dope in his organs. The summary says he was very healthy for a man his age." Wager shrugged. "He was robbed, yes. But robbers don't usually leave a note on the victim."

"So outside of that little drawing, we got a lot of nothing."

"Yessir."

Doyle pulled the drawing back across his desk, his square fingers tapping it lightly. "The Pueblo victim is unidentified, too. A white male, mid-to-late thirties, shot once in the heart with a large-caliber handgun. Robbery victim, but this was found stuck in his hand. Pueblo sent copies statewide to all agencies to see if it turned up anywhere else." The Bulldog's fingers stopped tapping. "Did we send a circular out?"

"No, sir. I should have."

Doyle nodded. "That's right, Wager. You should have. It was sloppy not to. So do it now. Start working from this angle." He tapped the drawing again. "It's the same m.o. and looks like the same kind of drawing. See what the lab can come up with on the picture you found. Get in touch with . . ." he read from a letter ". . . Detective Orvis down in Pueblo and see if he has any other replies to his circular."

"Yessir."

Doyle's fingers tapped again, holding Wager in the chair a moment longer. "I don't know how it was in Narcotics, Wager; but in Homicide, routine can be good and it can be bad. It's good when it makes you work systematically and cover all the bases. It's bad when it makes you think every murder's just another day at the office. You understand?"

"Yessir."

Doyle was right: Wager had screwed up, and the anger he felt was at himself. Back at his own desk he called Baird in the lab. "Have you run any tests on that angel drawing yet?"

"Let's see . . . No, we haven't got to it. I was hoping we'd get an i.d. to work with before we did any more on that one. We got about eight cases pending with viable suspects."

"Doyle wants the tests run as soon as you can."

"Crap. Well, the chief gets what he wants, doesn't he?" Baird added, "I can tell you one thing about it without any tests, though."

"What's that?"

"It's a copy. Xerox, maybe. But a plain-paper copier was used. I took it out of the evidence bag and looked at it in the light. You can see the difference in the embossing."

"A Xerox? It looked real to me."

"It is real. But it's not an original. It just looks like an original. Hell, some of these new copiers can photograph a dollar bill close enough to fool a change machine. My son told me some of the kids in his junior high are working that little scam."

A copy. There could be tens of copies. Hundreds.

"I don't think the paper's going to tell us much," said Baird. "We already dusted it for prints, of course, but there weren't any. I'd have let you know if there were."

"Do what you can."

"I always do."

His next call was through the WATS line to Pueblo, one of the string of growing cities that ran down the east face of the Rockies from Wyoming to New Mexico. All Wager could remember of the town was the wall of towering steel blast furnaces and the mountains of coal piles that lined I-25 as it arced past the small and usually hot and dusty city. After two or three voices he finally reached Detective Orvis.

"This is Detective Wager, Denver Police, Homicide. I'm calling about that inquiry you sent out—the angel with the sword."

"Right! Do you have anything for us?"

"A similar killing. And a similar drawing."

The line clicked somewhere in the muffled distance. "A white male? One shot in the heart? Possible robbery motive?"

"And no identification yet. Has anyone else called you?"

"No, no . . . You're the first "

Wager understood why Orvis said "first"; the idea of multiple murders had crossed his mind, too, when he talked to Baird. "Is your drawing a Xerox copy?"

"Yeah. That's why I sent out an inquiry. How about yours?"

"It's a copy, too." He gave Orvis the date and circumstances of his John Doe killing. "Let me know if you get an i.d. on yours—or anything else. I'll give you my office and home number."

"Fine. You're the case officer up there?"

Wager noted the stress on "up there"; Orvis was telling him that it was his case, too; that the Denver PD might be the state's biggest department, but it had no jurisdiction in Pueblo. "Right. Me and Detective Axton." He spelled Max's name. "We'll keep you informed of what we come up with."

After he hung up, Wager finished the list of Ellison's known associates and phoned them to Records and the Crime Information Center for any addresses they might have. Then he and Axton would start down the list and shake trees until some clue fell out. But the real thing on his mind was that angel and sword. One here; one in Pueblo. Maybe one or more in other states, too.

He stared across the empty desks at the cream-colored wall of the pleasantly quiet office. Controlled acoustics. Controlled temperature and humidity. Carefully neutral in color scheme. Space for each desk measured by some engineer and the square footage written into the building design. But as much as the old headquarters building had depressed him with its indelible dirt, its confusion of noises and crowded bustle, it had seemed closer to the street than this shadowless and efficient box. Perhaps it was only a matter of time before this newness wore off—before the snarled clutter of the street gradually worked its way up the muted elevators, up the wide and carpeted stairwells, to glide like gritty fog into this room with its hermetically sealed windows. A little of it had to come in each time a detective strode through that door; a pinch, a wisp, a slight odor hanging in the creases of a jacket, trailing from the worn rubber heel of a shoe. It was a matter of degree, a matter of balance between order and confusion. But as yet too much order dominated this new office and made him uneasy. One could stay up here and forget the disorder that swirled through the streets outside the building.

Restless, he stood and looked past the tinted glass down at the rectangles of streets and alleys. To the south of the new police building the roofs were kept low by city ordinance so that people strolling in the parks on the east side could have an unobstructed view of the mountains. Elsewhere thirty- and forty-story towers thrust up to glint in the sun. And everywhere the fragile web of cranes swung gently over new excavations. More office buildings, more commuter space, fewer homes to fill the evening streets with the glow of living-room lights. The city was becoming as functional as a draftsman's sketch. The starkly efficient plans of engineers, backed by the irresistible pressure of oil money, were creating a new city of smooth plastic façades.

From up here even the older section, the less-developed swatch of stubby apartment buildings and small houses, seemed as clean and regular as the face of a waffle iron. What would be left to erupt in a city as orderly and functional as a dynamo? What cries or songs would fill the vacant night streets between the empty skyscrapers of the future? Wager, his vision of the future blurred with doubt, did not believe that all happened for the best. It just happened. And if he often hated the things that belched rage and pain into the streets, he also loved the excitement and heat of it. It was a paradox he occasionally wondered about in the silent times in his apartment—how one could love the thing he hated and hate the thing he loved. He was drawn to the street and its hungers up to a point—the point when those hungers became chaos.

Denver did have its share of truly weird ones, those who moved far beyond excitement in order to open doors to subterranean terrors. Some drifted in from Texas or New Jersey on their way to LA, where they settled in like ticks to start a religion or a revolution. Some were homegrown —native talent to be proud of, like the kid who thumped his roommate to death with a ball peen hammer and then carved him up and wrapped the bits and pieces in neat packages, which he distributed around the neighborhood. Or the woman who went just a tad too far into chemically induced ecstasy and burned her mother to death so the smoke could carry her prayers to heaven. And there was the series of half a dozen killings of young women—rape, strangle, and dump—that was still on the open file, without even a suspect to watch. Those were the ones that made killings like that of the garroted Ellison seem as routine and familiar as tying a shoe.

Perhaps Denver was no longer to be spared the kind of mass murderer who surfaced in other corners of the country—the Zebra killers of California, some of whom were still at large and still preaching revenge against whites; the Texas murders of forty girls and women—still no suspect a decade later; Gacy in Chicago; the Atlanta ghoul who fed on black children; the Zodiac killer of San Francisco, never caught even with a description of the suspect and the notes left behind for the police—a cross in a circle. The Zodiac notes had not been Xeroxed, and the victims had been chosen at random—which added an even scarier note, as if the black edge of the careless universe had been touched.

One of the things Wager liked about his job was that while doing it he sought—and often found—reasons behind an act of insane savagery. Sometimes it was only insanity—temporary or otherwise—a term that comfortably covered a lot of explanations in the eyes of the law. But it was an explanation, though a weak one; it re-established the line between confusion and coherence. The law—people like Wager who served the law—traced that line, and maybe it was part of the burden of his occupation that he could see both sides of that line. But he always felt a personal victory when he could explain the motive of an act, even if in terms of insanity. His job was to claim some territory for coherence, even if that effort had once led him to claim more than the law allowed. And in claiming, to lose a partner's trust. But of late the territory of chaos seemed to grow larger, while Wager's victories were smaller and smaller in the face of a threat that loomed like the coming night sky. An angel holding a sword. Somehow that message towered over the usual chaos of the street: manslaughter, family slayings, garrotings—even these were dwarfed by that little drawing. Because whoever committed that murder acted from reason, but a reason founded on, and growing out of, the same vast insanity that brought wars—a superstructure of coherence that gathered more and more followers, those who never looked to see that their belief was founded on insanity.

Cross-in-circle, angel-and-sword. Wager caught himself assuming that there would be more angel killings. He could feel the promise of some kind of pattern in these killings, which was why he was certain there would be more: someone was following a path that led to specific victims. Those notes—symbols of the killer's triumph—were meant to be seen by future victims.

3.

The third angel came almost a week later as Wager, elbow-deep in a new set of time-study forms, tried to classify his activities for the previous six months into little boxes that the computer could scan. The little boxes indicated the number of cases handled, the types, the number of hours each demanded, the range of support areas utilized, and something called "other" which the computer couldn't break down into component parts. Then a highly paid consultant would come in and read the form that he had designed, point to the quantified evidence, and tell Doyle where his people were screwing up. Pretty soon they would be solving forms and not solving cases, because there was nothing to mark on the form that quantified the way victims looked and smelled or the wide-eyed numbness of relatives or the tight-lipped worry of arrested suspects. Those kinds of data couldn't be put into little boxes with a number two pencil, and to Wager's way of thinking there wasn't much of real importance that could be, except the number of cases pending and the

number of cases cleared. You didn't need a consultant or
a computer to figure that. But along with the department's
brand-new building had come new ways of administra-
tion, and instead of being out on the pavement with Axton
where he should be, he was here scratching paper. Wager
sighed and filled in another little square and moved to the
next query. This afternoon Max was to fill in his form and
Wager would make the rounds.

His telephone rang: the Bulldog. "Wager, another one
of those angel drawings came in the mail this morning.
Can you come up?"

"My time-study's due at noon, Chief," said Wager
sweetly. "You sent out a memo on it."

There was a slight pause. "That can wait."

"I'll be right there."

This time Chief Doyle's fingers tapped on his intercom
box while Wager read the letter that had come with the
copy of the sketch. The letterhead said "Grant County
Sheriff's Office, Loma Vista, Colo., 81321." It was a small
town on the Western Slope; Wager had driven through it
on a fishing trip years ago. The letter described the homicide and asked for any help DPD could give. It was signed
Daryl Tice, Sheriff.

"This is a little different from the other two," said
Wager.

"How's that?"

"They know who the victim is, for one thing."

Doyle nodded and gazed out the window. His view
looked across the shallow bowl of the South Platte toward
the front range of mountains with their newly cut construction scars orange in the morning sun. "There's probably no more than fifteen thousand people scattered
around that whole county. In a population that small, it
would be surprising if they didn't know everybody."

That made some sense, and besides, Wager had been a

cop long enough to know that any pattern he imagined might not be the one a criminal had in mind. True, this victim had been shot in the back of the head rather than in the heart, but the type of weapon was the same—a large-caliber handgun. "Was the angel Tice found a Xerox or an original?"

"You know as much as I do, Wager."

The letter didn't say. "I'll give him a call."

"Do that." Doyle didn't lean back as he usually did when a conference was over. Instead, his gaze stayed aimed at the window, holding Wager by its stillness. Finally he said what Wager had already thought. "That's number three. God knows how many more there might be." Then, "I take it you've got nothing more on our angel killing?"

"No, sir. Neither has Pueblo on theirs. I called Orvis to check just before coming up."

The Bulldog nodded and said, more to himself than to Wager, "Three in a month. All over the state." His eyes turned to Wager and he asked mildly, "What's this I read in the paper a few days ago—that article by Gargan on the barbed-wire strangling. Are you the homicide detective he meant when he called one of our people 'nasty, brutish, and short'?"

Wager stifled a grin. "He mailed a copy to me."

"I don't like that kind of relationship with the press. They've got their job and we've got ours. If we work together, it'll be easier on both of us. A personal animosity between the press and one officer can hurt us all, Wager."

"Gargan wanted information on that killing. I told him everything I knew at the time that wasn't classified. Just like the op manual says. He wasn't happy with it. Tough shit."

Doyle said "um" and his fingers started their light dance again. "Everybody's shorthanded. Us. Pueblo. Everybody."

That was true, but Wager wasn't sure what the Bulldog was working toward.

"But DPD's got the most people. We can best absorb a temporary loan."

Wager got the idea. "Why me? That Gargan thing?"

The Bulldog nodded. "He's on a special assignment by the *Post* to look into the whole Crimes Against Persons section, Wager, to enlighten the public why the serious crimes keep rising and the convictions keep falling. That means you two are going to run into each other. He's going to spend the next couple of days head-hunting, and I don't want you antagonizing him."

Doyle didn't want Wager to antagonize Gargan!

"Moreover," he went on, before Wager's open mouth could close around an angry word, "you and Axton are due for the night shift. We can get by with one man on the night shift for a day or two."

"It's my case," said Wager, unwilling to be shoved aside because of someone like Gargan.

"That's the real reason, isn't it?" Doyle agreed mildly. He picked up his telephone and punched a series of numbers. "Crowther? This is Doyle. I've got a man for special assignment outside the jurisdiction. Sure—he'll be right over." Hanging up, the Bulldog said to Wager, "Get over to Personnel; they'll issue your vouchers and certification. And Wager, you'll be pretty much on your own over there." Doyle leaned back in his chair like a man settling into a marshmallow. "But you like that, anyway."

"You're Detective Sergeant Wager, are you? The one they sent out to clear all this up." He made it sound more like a statement than a question. In time Wager learned that all of Sheriff Tice's questions came out that way, and that he expected them to be answered.

And in time the sheriff would learn that Wager didn't answer the dumb ones. He folded away his badge case. "Can you show me the victim's file?"

Tice heaved out of the chair, which creaked with relief. Behind him, anchored by a half-shut window and a frame of plywood, an air conditioner fluttered a short strip of cloth from its grill. The sheriff's offices, like almost every other building, were near the edge of the small town. Through the window, Wager saw the long arc of blue-green sagebrush, broken here and there by a mist of irrigation wheels and scattered ranch buildings. Somewhere beyond the etched horizon was the rugged benchland, cut by a small river, then the true desert leading into Utah. Then came a massive upsweep of earth that tilted into those mountain peaks so far away that only their summer snow glimmered low against the sky, like dimly seen clouds.

"You want some coffee first?"

It was part of the ritual between cops, even those whose trust of each other was only official. "Thanks."

Tice poured a cup from a Silex with glass sides stained brown. "Cream or sugar?"

"Black."

Black it was. And hot. And bitter. Routines might vary, faces might differ, settings might change, but the coffee in every police unit in the sovereign State of Colorado tasted the same. Wager sipped and waited for the sheriff to pour his own careful cup, the *tink* of his spoon light but sharp over the muffled radio traffic and typewriters in the outer office. Tice would take his time about showing Wager the file; when the sheriff had asked for help from DPD he'd meant information, but instead he was sent an outsider who looked like he wanted to poke his nose into Tice's business. Well Grant County was his county, and in his county things were done his way. And Wager would be patient; good manners would allow Tice to save some face.

"You have a good drive over?" The back of the sheriff's head was still toward him.

That wasn't what occupied Tice's mind, but Wager said "fine." Which was true: it had been fine—once out of the brown haze that settled over early-morning Denver and its noisy highways, up into the front range, and finally beyond the clusters of towns that now littered the freeway and threatened to join together into a single hundred-mile-long strip-city of booming alpine suburbia. It had been fine to turn off the broad concrete lanes of carefully engineered curves and get onto the network of secondary roads—the ones that twisted and bumped through narrow canyons or across empty valleys and past mile after mile of vacant grazing land or along shallow, bright streams that on this side of the Divide foamed toward the Colorado River. That had been the best part: to be reminded of the vast spaces that still hung silently between mountain peaks, of the variety of shades of green that covered valleys and slopes up as far as the nude and snow-freckled rock above timberline. To be reminded, too, that not all of Colorado was booming, with a new skyscraper every week, a new subdivision every month, another Fastest-Growing-Little-City-in-the-Country report. "It was a nice drive," Wager said.

"What was it—five hours? Six? You could've flown," said Tice. "It's less than an hour to Denver. We got a new county airport put in—all-weather tower, night illumination. Had to have it for the oil shale people." He finished stirring his coffee with a final *tink* and put the spoon in its own empty cup. "Come on," he said. "You'll want a place to look over the file." He did not ask how long Wager planned to stay, and Wager did not tell him.

Leading back through the outer office, Tice introduced him to the clerks. "This here's Detective Sergeant Wager from Denver. He's come to help out with the Mueller case, so I want you people to give him whatever he needs."

The office staff for the Grant County sheriff's office: a very nice-looking brunette wearing tight jeans and shuffling through a file drawer, a not-as-nice-looking bleached blond thumping a typewriter, and an older woman in slacks monitoring the radio and telephones while she, too, typed. They smiled collectively at Wager, who nodded back and said hello. He had no doubt that they'd known who he was before he walked through the door. They might or might not have known that it wasn't Tice's decision that brought Wager to them.

"We cleared a table for you back here, Detective Wager." The sheriff pointed to a room larger than a breadbox but smaller than a closet. Freshly outlined marks on the floor showed that filing cabinets had been shoved aside to make space for the small table that looked back blankly. "It's the best we could do. The department needs a whole new building, but we don't have a hope of one for the next five years. By then," Tice's shoulders rose and fell in a heavy sigh of promised contentment, "I'll be retired, and somebody else can fight with the county commissioners."

"This is fine," said Wager.

"Make yourself to home. I'll get the file."

It was a manila folder with the familiar red tag for an unsolved case. On the lip, penned carefully with the foreknowledge that this folder would get a lot more traffic than most, was the name "Mueller, Herman F." The investigating officer's report was the top sheet; beneath that were depositions, statements, coroner's report, receipts, correspondence of one type or another, and a smaller envelope of Polaroid photographs. Wager would look more closely at those later.. He began with the officer's report. Herman Frederick Mueller. b. St. Louis, Mo., Mar. 19, 1931 ... Wager scanned the victim's history and the crime report for facts that he did not already have from Tice's earlier letter. When the entries conflicted, he checked his little green notebook and made the corrections. In the section of the report headed "Statement of Circumstances," he found the item that had led him to Loma Vista: placed between the first and second fingers of the victim's left hand was a folded slip of paper bearing the sketch of an angel holding a sword.

The paper itself would be in the sheriff's evidence locker; after he finished studying the file, Wager copied down Mueller's case number and wandered back into the busy main office, where he stood waiting. The women hesitated before the pretty brunette smiled and said, "Can I get you something?"

Like the others, she wore no name tag. "I need an item from your evidence locker."

"The what? Oh—the safe! Sure." She led him to the large Mosler that blocked one corner of the room. The heavy door hung open and, without glancing at the file number Wager held, she rummaged through the middle shelf to pull out a flat brown envelope. "Here you go—the Mueller case, right?"

"Yeah, right. You want me to sign for it?"

She shook her head, brown eyes wide with curiosity. "What for?"

"You don't require people to sign evidence in and out?"

"No. We're always here. And when we're not, the safe's locked."

"What's your name?"

"Cynthia."

"Thanks, Cynthia."

"And your name's Gabriel. Or do you want to be called Officer Wager?"

Her eyes teased and he smiled back. "Gabe. Only angels are called Gabriel."

"And you're no angel?"

"I just work for them," he joked.

The laughter went out of her eyes, blown by a sudden gust of fright that she quickly hid behind a taut smile. "We're all on the side of the angels," she said, and turned away with the smile carefully held in place, leaving Wager puzzled. He stared a long moment before he went back to his small table.

There he matched the sheriff's evidence with his own copy of the sketch. Under the magnifying glass they looked identical, which wasn't surprising since both were Xerox copies. Turning to the photographs of the victim and the supporting documents of the case, he set aside Cynthia's unexplained fright and gradually lost himself in the awkwardly precise language of reports. After a while, as he neared the bottom of the stack of papers, the silence behind him became noticeable: the clatter and ding of typing had ceased, the telephone noises quieted, and only the occasional snap and chatter of the radio filled the sheriff's offices. Wager gave a long sigh, put Tice's evidence back in its plastic Baggie, and tucked his own copy of the angel away in his small green notebook.

"Is the sheriff in?"

Apparently Communications took her lunch break after the others; the older woman looked up from her log of radio messages and nodded at the sheriff's door. "Just go right in."

Tice was poking with a ball-point pen at a small stack of papers. "You got it solved yet?"

If it was a joke, it wasn't funny; if it was sarcasm, Wager

could do without it. He set the plastic Baggie on the sheriff's desk. "This should go back in your evidence locker." Pointing to the sketch, Wager asked, "Does the drawing mean anything to you?"

"First, we don't have an evidence locker, Detective Wager. All's we got is a safe. And second, no, that angel don't mean a thing to me. But it does to some damn fools. Or so they claim."

Such as his own clerk, Cynthia. "What do they claim?"

"There's some around the county that believe in the avenging angels. I don't happen to."

"What's the avenging angels?"

The man heaved back in his protesting chair and eyed Wager. "You're not Mormon I guess. I thought DPD sent you over because you were supposed to know all about this shooting."

"They sent me over to learn about it, Tice. That's what I'm trying to do."

"I see—learn." He grunted. "You a Catholic? You raised a Catholic?"

Wager nodded shortly; he preferred to ask the questions.

"Got any Mormons over on the Eastern Slope?" Tice asked.

"Latter-Day Saints? Sure."

Tice grunted again. "LDS—some of them don't like to be called Mormons, and some Mormons don't like to be called LDS."

When Wager was a kid, all non-Catholics were lumped under the heading "black Prods," and either were pitied or laughed at because they had traded religion for superstition. There were even a few fights over who was the most Christian. But for a long time now all the sects and their jealousies had made no difference to him, and it was hard to imagine people getting upset over rituals. "What's this got to do with the picture?"

"You were sent here to learn you say? You want to learn or not?"

Wager picked at an imaginary piece of lint on his trousers and managed to hold his temper. "Go on."

"I aim to." Tice waited for Wager to say something more, but he didn't. "Now out here we got people scattered over the benchland that don't like either bunch because they think they're the only real Mormons left. They're the ones that still believe in the avenging angels or destroying angels or sons of Dan or whatever you want to call them."

"Why?"

"Because the Mormon church used to have avenging angels, and these people stay with the old ways. They're the ones that think Negroes are Satan's children—that's why their skin's black; and that Indians are red because they broke God's commandments. And that polygamy's still one of God's laws. They're what you might call your basic, hard-shelled, unreformed Mormons."

"Polygamy?"

"You going to tell me that's against the law?" The sheriff had that look of a man who'd argued the question before and was damned if he wanted to go over the same ground again.

"I don't have to tell you that."

"No. You don't. But around here we got people living together without marriage, we got people living together that are still married to somebody else, and we got people living together that are married to each other—except there's more than one woman that's married to the same man. As far as I know, we don't yet have two men married to each other, not like they do over in Boulder. But we got a few of that kind living together that ain't married. We got a whole variety of connubial bliss in these mountains, Detective Wager. Maybe it's something in the water. But as long as those people don't endanger life or property, I don't bother them."

"You have any men and women that are just married to each other?"

Tice coughed something like a laugh. "A few. They seem to be the unhappiest of the lot."

"What's the avenging angels have to do with it?"

"Nothing—it has to do with Mormons. The avenging angels were Mormon vigilantes. When Brigham Young started to settle groups of Mormons in the corridor down from Salt Lake City to San Diego, California, they ran into people who didn't like Mormons. Some were on the land first, like around here; some tried to move in after the Mormons did the improving. Brigham Young sent out a chosen few to convert or kill off anybody they couldn't buy out. And to go after any Mormons who wanted to stray from Brigham's path. Since Brigham spoke for God, these vigilantes were just doing what God told them to, so they were called avenging angels or Danites or what-all."

"And . . . ?"

Tice shrugged. "There were some killings by Mormons around here. Massacres just west of here. But that was a long time ago—a hundred years. And it was kept pretty secret even then. I doubt you find many Mormons today that know much about them. Sure as hell few that believe in them."

Wager looked at the drawing spread in its plastic wrapper. "Mueller was one of these unreformed Mormons then?"

"No, he wasn't. I can't find any link between him and any kind of Mormon or any other religion. As far as I can learn, he spent his Sundays—Saturdays, too—getting drunk by himself up in his cabin. Your Mormons of all kinds aren't supposed to drink coffee even, let alone whiskey. They do drink a lot of soda pop," he added. "The kind the church is a major stockholder in."

"No other motive? Robbery?"

"Hell, Mueller never had a thing but that cabin and maybe a few hundred acres of timberland around it. When he needed a little cash, he'd hire out as a hand. Most of the time he didn't even bother with that. Look, Detective Wager, I may be just a county sheriff, but by God I been in law enforcement work almost thirty years. I know enough about this business to look for the motive in a killing. And I can't find one in the Mueller case—no enemies, no robbery, no relatives, no mysterious avenging angels."

"But there is that drawing. According to the investigating deputy—Roy Yates?—it was folded up and stuck between Mueller's fingers so it wouldn't be missed." Wager half shrugged at the obviousness of it. "That fits the m.o. of the Denver killing, and that angel's an exact copy of the ones we found in Denver and Pueblo."

Tice sighed. "Yeah." Then he grabbed his Stetson from a corner of his desk and grunted to his feet. "There is that damn picture, and there are some damn fools it scares hell out of. Come on—let's get some lunch. Yates should be down from Rio Piedra in an hour or so and then you can worry him about it. Whenever I get puzzled I get hungry, and that damn picture's ruining my diet."

Openness. That was the word Wager searched for in his mind when a relaxed and belching Tice led him from the restaurant and around town by way of introduction. The people on the streets had none of that squinty-eyed I'm-as-good-as-you-are look that so many newcomers to Denver assumed after they'd been out west for six months. Instead these people assumed that, since Wager didn't have long hair, he was as good as they were, and they would treat him that way unless he proved otherwise. It was the kind of easy acceptance he remembered in his old neighborhood, before the bulldozers leveled it first for parking lots, then for the blank glass faces of classrooms and office buildings. Here, the openness in attitude matched the openness of the ranch and farmland scattered across the broad plateau between the steep crest of eastern mountains and the long, falling distances to the western horizon. It was an openness that was emphasized by the hardness of the afternoon sunlight, which glowed as much from the earth as from the sky. Even Deputy Yates, to whom he was introduced when they got back to the sheriff's office, and who was to take him out to Mueller's ranch, seemed genuinely glad after a few moments of cautious sniffing—two dogs of the same breed meeting for the first time—to tell Wager all he knew about the homicide and everything else.

"That kind of thing doesn't happen much in this neck of the woods, Gabe."

Tice had introduced him as Gabe Wager from DPD, and Yates went right to his first name. Which was friendlier than Tice was and all right with Wager. "Not many homicides in the county?"

"Nope. We get some shootings, suicides and accidents mostly. One or two a year. And if we do get a homicide, it's because of a fight; somebody gets beat up in a bar and wants to get even, or somebody messes with another man's woman." Yates turned the four-wheel-drive car onto the bumpy state road that led back north to Rio Piedra and Mueller's isolated ranch. "Burglary's the big thing around here—we're starting to get transient construction workers coming in, and they'll rip off whatever ain't tied down. Dope, too." He bobbed his head toward the jagged snow-covered peaks fifty miles away. "The ski people bring that in. But the marshal up there won't move against them. He calls it the 'community life-style.'" Yates slapped his palm against the steering wheel. "He says those people hired him, and those people's standards are what he's paid to uphold." He added, "No matter how low."

"What about the DA? Doesn't the marshal have to report to the district attorney?"

Yates's yellow-brown eyes glanced from the narrow highway toward Wager, unsure just how much might be repeated and to whom. "Our DA don't like to prosecute. He don't like us spending our time in court when we should be on the road or serving warrants, he says. Besides, he's a Republican, and the marshal's a Democrat. They don't work together too well."

The deputy was a lean man in his thirties whose Adam's apple bobbed prominently when he talked. Beneath his tan uniform shirt, trimmed with western piping on back and chest, the faint outline of straps and ridges showed that he wore body armor. Most of the street cops in Denver wore it, too, but there it seemed necessary. "What about the sheriff's office? How does Tice get along with the DA?"

"Not too good. Tice wants to provide law enforcement for the unincorporated areas of the county—which is most of it. The DA thinks the sheriff should spend his time serving papers and running the jail. We make a little money on papers and prisoners."

"How in hell does the DA get any convictions?"

"Guilty pleas on reduced charges, mostly. He says it serves justice and the county budget at the same time. Besides, he's a good buddy of the leading defense lawyer in town. I won't say there's any pay-offs, but if you ever get charged with something, there's one lawyer who can get you out of it without ever going to trial."

As in every judicial district in Colorado, the DA decided which cases to prosecute and how hard to go after them. Plea bargaining could save the state a lot of money and the prosecutor a lot of work, as Kolagny, the Denver prosecuting attorney, knew. And if you only went after the sure cases, you could have a very good conviction rate, one that the state's attorney general would be happy with. "It sounds like a real circus, Roy. How about the municipal police? How do you get along with them?"

"There's only one municipality in the county—Loma Vista. The rest of the towns have marshals, and some are good and some are bad. As far as the Loma Vista police is concerned, it depends on who's got duty. If you need backup, your friends come when you holler. The others don't." He told Wager about a bar fight during one of the region's summer tourist celebrations, Gold Rush Days: two sheriff's officers sent to quell a brawl of thirty drunken construction workers and not-too-sober cowboys. "Municipal didn't send anybody into the county to help with that one. We ended up standing outside the door and picking them up when they flew out. If there'd been just four or five of us, we could have gone in and broken it up. But just the two of us, and one of them a reserve . . ." Yates tried to answer Wager's silence. "Look, Gabe, the s.o. has three full-timers for the whole county, including Tice. We're not as rich as Cortez or Grand Junction. We just don't have the tax base for a good sheriff's office. If I spend two, three days on a court case, I'm not out on calls, like I should be. And I'll tell you what, if we don't respond to calls, Sheriff Tice don't get re-elected, and I don't get reappointed. That's just the way it is out here."

Out here, back there, anywhere and everywhere, the

sure conviction of criminals was the best prevention a law agency could offer. Proving your case in court was what it was all about, and if a DA took only the easy wins, the real crooks would get a lot smarter a lot faster. Wager gazed out the window at a flooded meadow whose grass was so green it was almost black against the blue of water-reflected sky. He was here on *one* case. As an outsider. He wanted to remember that. And Yates, like any good cop, preferred to be on the street instead of in court or filling out time-study forms. Even if things were done differently or downright wrong in Grant County, he wanted to remember that.

"Were you born around here?"

"Texas. El Paso. Worked for the s.o. in El Paso County for two years before coming up here. I been here almost ten years now. Man, talk about your budget—that El Paso s.o. had helicopters, take-home vehicles, overtime pay, everything! It cost me almost three hundred a month to come up here." He pointed out the window by way of explanation. "But it was worth it—I like the country."

Looking where Yates pointed, Wager could understand. It was the kind of scenery people traveled thousands of miles and paid hundreds of dollars to see. And Yates, assigned to live in the northwest corner of the county as the sole resident peace officer, would be his own boss most of the time. It was the kind of job a city cop might like to retire to. If he could stand the small-town politics. Gazing at those steep snowfields brilliant in the afternoon sun, Wager figured the years to his own retirement. He was about halfway there, and it wouldn't be bad at all to move out to a place like this. "How many people in the county?"

Yates thought a moment. "Last census said a little over two thousand, outside Loma Vista. About twenty thousand in all. But it was wrong—I figure another five hundred, maybe more. I know a dozen new families up in my corner that have moved in from God-knows-where." He grinned, wrinkling his flat cheeks. "A real population explosion."

A pickup truck passed with a large tank filling the bed. The driver raised a hand and Yates waved back. Wager tried to remember the last time he saw someone in Denver lift a friendly hand to a cop.

"That's Deputy Hodges's uncle—looks like he's going for a load of water."

"Water?" They were climbing swiftly now; the wet meadow was left behind as the road lifted through piñon and scrub to the top of a mesa. But the grass was still green and fresh, and narrow gullies cut in the mesa showed that creeks ran from those distant snowfields. "It seems wet enough."

"It's spotty, and some areas are downright dry. Water rights! It's the biggest damned headache we have, and the water laws in this state are a lawyer's delight. Subsurface water, too; it's a whole new area and nobody really knows what the law is. We're always serving summonses on water rights cases."

The road swerved in sharp curves as it dipped and rose again, this time into a pine-filled valley that was formed by the lowest ridges of the mountain range. Among the tree trunks scattered vacation cabins sat awaiting another brief season; occasional trucks and cars passed with a wave, and Yates seemed to know most of the drivers. Wager let him talk without interruption and gazed at the passing landscape. On the radio, infrequent coded messages crackled with the slow business of the sheriff's office, the municipal police in Loma Vista behind them, the faint queries and answers of the county's highway maintenance crews. Yates slowed suddenly to swerve onto a graded dirt road —"Got a paper to serve, won't take long"—and groped his automobile down first one narrow dirt track and then another, looking for the plastic lot number nailed to a pine tree. Not all of the empty-looking A-frames or log cabins were vacation homes; Wager caught glimpses of pickup trucks with current Colorado plates, of large dogs sitting up to stare as the vehicle rattled past, of the occasional child playing alone around the cinder-block foundation of a half-hidden mobile home.

"Here we are," said the deputy, and he guided the four-wheel drive along a twisty two-rut road that ended in a littered clearing before a barn-shaped log house. A woman stood behind the screen door and peered out cautiously. Unhurried, Yates checked out of the radio net and took the brown envelope with the summons. "Be just a minute," he said to Wager; then, "Morning, ma'am," to the silent woman.

"He was lying in that corner facedown." Yates had steered the vehicle up a jolting path and across a soft meadow. Tucked beneath the pines fringing the open space sat a small cabin built of dark logs and railroad ties and roofed with rusting sheet metal. A rain-speckled cardboard sign was nailed to the door: CRIME SCENE KEEP OUT UNDER PENALTY OF THE LAW. D. L. TICE GRANT COUNTY SHERIFF. A still-shiny chain and padlock dangled across the door; Yates found the key and unlocked it and let Wager into the single room cluttered with the years of debris of a man's isolated life. On plank shelves spiked along one wall, piles of old magazines and newspapers slowly yellowed; a black iron stove, used for both heating and cooking, sat with its firebox door sagging open; a half-dozen pots and pans hung within easy reach. Over a steel sink resting in an iron frame, a pump nozzle drooped; the corners of the room were crammed with cardboard boxes holding tools, license plates going back thirty years, scraps of electric wire and baling cord, jars and cans of food, old clothes that smelled of stale dirt, letters and legal papers dating from the 1940s and brittle to the touch. A twisting avenue led from the front door to a large sofa, its upholstery split, past a tassled lamp, to the rumpled blankets of the sheetless mattress, to a table whose planks were cleared at one end for use and whose other end was crammed with more magazines, an old clock, a pad of Indian Head lined paper, pencil stubs, an old-fashioned radio with a cathedral front, and dishes and tin silverware, more or less clean, and finally to the stove sagging beneath its rusty chimney pipe.

"He was one old packrat, wasn't he?" Yates said. "I had to inventory this whole pile of crap."

Wager had seen a copy of the wearisome long list in the victim's file. He sidled down the aisle looking at this and that. "How'd you find out about him?"

"He had a job to do over at the Lazy J ranch—fencing, roofing; when he was more than a couple days late, Mr. Connell, the ranch manager, came over and found him."

So Mueller had been dead for a couple of days before he was discovered. That explained the lingering and half-familiar odor that blended with the general damp mustiness of the cabin. Wager studied the corner Yates had pointed out. It was behind the table and away from the door. He knew from the crime report that Mueller had been shot once in the back of the head with a large-caliber weapon, probably a pistol, and that the slug had not been found either in the body or in the log walls.

"You didn't outline the body with chalk?"

Even in the dim light of the unshaded ceiling bulb, Wager could see Yates's sallow neck turn red with embarrassment. "Where the hell would I get chalk? I took pictures, is what I did. You seen the pictures, didn't you? That shows you where the body was."

You couldn't measure distances from a picture; you couldn't get as clear an idea of the body's position, either. But Wager nodded silently and stepped carefully to a location that might have been where the killer stood when he fired into the man's head. Given the narrow alleys between boxes and piles, there weren't many other places the gunman could have stood. In one of the railroad ties, near eye level, three or four gouges showed freshly splintered wood. "Is that where you looked for the slug?"

Yates said yes. "I stood right where you're standing, Gabe—I figure that's where the killer stood. And then I went and dug into every hole in that wall. I even used a metal detector on the floor and along the chinks. But all I found were nails and screws and such."

He expected Wager to tell him he did the right thing. "That was the right thing to do."

"Well I didn't need chalk for something like that."

"But the slug should still be here somewhere."

"I looked. Sheriff Tice looked. Even the coronor. Every crack in the logs, floor, even the roof. The only thing we can figure is it angled off Mueller's skull and out that window." He pointed to the small hinged square of panes. "It was open. I had to close it to keep varmints out."

Wager eyed the screenless window from where he stood. It was a possibility—faint, but possible. If the killer had stood over by the stove, the possibility was more likely, but the location of the body wasn't quite right for that. And the coroner's report said the body had not been moved.

"Did you go over the place for fingerprints?" Wager lifted the cover on the Indian Head pad to reveal a penciled scrawl of numbers and a painfully totaled column reading $24,974.00, heavily underlined twice.

"Yep. But the only good ones found was Mueller's. The front door was messed up—everybody coming in the place put their hand to the latch." He watched Wager scan the tablet. "That make any sense to you?"

"Just numbers. Income, payment, who knows?" He looked around the jumble of the room. "You found no other recent documents? Nothing to show what he was figuring on?"

"Only that angel drawing."

Wager nodded.

"You want to look around outside?"

He followed Yates back into a sunshine which, after the dimness of the cabin, needled the eyes with glare. A worn path led around the corner to an outhouse that tilted forward enough to hang the slatted door open to reveal its empty bench. A black Dodge pickup, 1950s vintage, sat at the end of two well-worn ruts beside the cabin. A large spread of oil-soaked earth showed where Mueller habitually worked on the rusted truck.

"You couldn't find any tire impressions or footprints?"

"It'd rained."

"You have any guesses why he was shot?"

"Just that drawing. Mueller didn't have a damn thing anybody'd want. You can't graze a goat on most of his acreage, and the timber's not worth that much either. Nobody figures he had any money to hide, and he wasn't tortured or nothing, like somebody was trying to make him talk. Besides, the place looked just like it does now— it's a mess, but it's not tore up like somebody was looking for something. I've tried and I've tried, Gabe, but all I come up with is that angel."

And Wager had seen enough.

On the way back to Loma Vista Wager finally asked, "What can you tell me about the avenging angels?"

Yates concentrated on the highway's snaking, downhill curves. "Mister, you might laugh. I know Sheriff Tice does. But I believe in them."

"Why?"

"Because most of the people around here believe in them. If they believe, by God, so do I."

He tried to follow the deputy's reasoning. "Suppose they believe in Bigfoot or flying saucers?"

Yates's yellow-brown eyes slanted his way. "I'd have to go along with them, Gabe. I mean, look, I been here almost ten years; same northern half of the county, same roads, same patrols, damn near the same pay. But every day I find out something new about the people around here. We got folks living back in the hills or over on that benchland that've been here since Christ wore diapers. Some of them don't even send their kids to school because they don't want nothing to do with the state. Others I just know about from the county tax rolls, and they never call on the law or anybody else for a damn thing. If they get into a hassle they settle it themselves and nobody comes running to me about it." He braked slightly and glided around a fishhook bend. "And I don't go out bothering them if there's no call to. I guess what I'm trying to say is that things go on around here that I never see and a lot of times never even hear of. And some of the families that have been in these hills since before Colorado was a state were on the side of, or fought against, the avenging angels when the Mormons moved in here. They're the ones that act like the angels are real. Some of them are scared shitless, I swear."

It still sounded like a lot of crap to Wager. "Tice said he found no connection at all between Mueller and any Mormon group."

"That's right. I never heard of any either. But like I say, Gabe: there's a hell of a lot about these people that I plain don't know. And just because I don't know something, I'm not about to say it's impossible."

They rode in silence until the deputy turned the Jeep onto a paved county road leading into a narrow valley. "I'll run you through Rio Piedra—it's not too far out of the way. You might as well get the fifty-cent tour."

The valley twisted close to a stream that foamed whitely until the walls of pine and aspen opened; then it stilled into dark pools behind weathered beaver dams. Wide, shallow pools like these used to be Wager's favorite fishing spots, and he half wished he had brought the rod and reel and tackle box that were gathering dust in his apartment closet. He remembered how the trout could be seen as dark, hovering shadows halfway across a pond, and how you had to keep low and move gently to get close enough for a cautious flick of the light line, a gentle touch of the fly on the still surface.

"We get good fishing along here earlier in the spring. Fish and Game stocks this area. By now the tourists have about cleaned it out; it's too close to the road and all."

"I see."

The valley began to widen, and up ahead Wager spotted a road sign with two nameplates on one pole, RIO PIEDRA. Among the trees a handful of buildings made up the town: a worn gas station whose rusty pumps stuck out of a muddy drive like tree stumps, a windowless board building converted from a storage shed to a café with a pink Coors sign hanging on the closed door, some log cabins black with time and dampness that, except for woodsmoke, looked abandoned. Dirt roads led off to either side toward more thin trails and half-hidden cabins.

"My hometown," said Yates. "Actually I got an A-frame up on the side of the mountain there—gets a lot more sun than down here." He waved a hand at the shaggy mountain flank that still caught the lowering glow.

"How in hell do these people make a living?"

"Some work for the county—road crews, school-bus drivers. Some of them take in each other's wash, I guess. And we got some goddamn hippies that live off food stamps and rich parents. A couple of them are okay, but most ain't worth a damn." He pointed to the shadowed mountainside, where tongues of broken rock spilled down the slopes, and sagging mine buildings crumbled slowly. "Used to be a pretty big place in the 1890s—ten, twenty thousand people working the mines and services. Some of these people were born here and never left. God alone knows why."

To Wager, the remnants of the town were more lonely than the empty forest surrounding it. There, in the sprawling national forest, you expected isolation; and anyone found there was a transient fragment of humanity, with ties to someplace else where there were people. But here, the pitted stone foundations poked like rotted teeth above the weeds, and the time-stained cabins that remained were like stray seeds that cling to the poorest soil simply because that's where chance dropped them and they took hold. "You like living here?"

"Tell you the truth, Gabe, I'd a hell of a lot rather be down in Loma Vista. Me and the wife both. But here's where I'm stationed, and God knows the rent's cheap. Besides, it ain't as empty as it looks—there's maybe eighty, a hundred people in all, counting the ones back in the woods." Yates swung the vehicle roughly across a stony lot and headed back down the valley. "And this place might come back again, too."

"You mean the mines?"

"No, I think they're pretty much played out. They're mostly silver, anyway, and the price isn't that high. No, I mean oil shale—they found oil shale not too far away on the benchland, and this is the closest town if they ever start to develop it."

"Any Mormons around here?"

"They're mostly over the pass on the desert side. I don't know, there may be a few in this valley. No Mormon stake house, though. That's what they call their meetinghouse. No church of any kind, as a matter of fact." The deputy pushed the vehicle through the gears. "Let me get you back to Loma Vista before dark."

4.

The deputy's Jeep pulled away into the early dusk. Wager stood a moment outside the cinder-block sheriff's offices and watched the boxy vehicle go down the single main street. Two traffic lights shone brightly on the almost-vacant avenue, and over it all the wide sky was dark with evening cumulus clouds and a green twilight. In Denver, Wager didn't often get a chance to see a sky like that, and this minute of stillness reminded him of when his father had died. When he had learned that neither trees nor earth nor sky nor anything beyond would give him the slightest answer. This absolute indifference had frightened him when he first discovered it; now it was simply another statement of the isolation that all shared until, still alone, one faced death. But if every man's death would come when it would, it was Wager's job to hunt down those who hastened death for others. He wasn't being paid to stand in the street and gaze at a darkening sky, or to feel this embarrassing return of some forgotten childhood fear.

Nonetheless, he gazed a moment more; but the twilight had drained of meaning and become just a fading color.

Centuries ago some Anasazi—some local cliff dweller—
had probably stood and watched the same shading of
green into purple and black, and heard the same raucous
squawk of the wheeling nighthawks. And perhaps the
Anasazi asked the same questions—and received the same
silence in return. It was nothing new.

Inside the now-quiet sheriff's offices, a different woman
sat at the radio console, the clipboard of logged calls
propped in front of her, a photo-filled *National Enquirer*
spread on the desk beside it.

"Hi," she said. "Can I help you?"

"Is Sheriff Tice around?"

"He's home, but I can get him on the radio if it's an
emergency." She peered closely. "Are you Detective
Wager? From Denver?"

Wager nodded.

"I'm D.L.'s daughter-in-law. He told me to tell you that
he reserved a room at the Mesaland Motel if you need it
—he was worried they'd be filled up before you got back.
Do you want to talk to him? His home number's right
here." She pointed to a sheet taped to the desk top.

"It's not that important. Can I use this phone? For an
official call?"

"Sure." She watched him settle behind one of the secre-
taries' desks with a polite smile of approval until he started
to dial; then she turned back to her gossip sheet to show
Wager that she wasn't at all interested in what he had to
say.

Max should be awake by now. Eating, probably. He
went on duty at midnight, and when Wager had that shift
he was always up and messing around by seven. He gave
the operator his Denver office number and the code that
let him charge the call to DPD, then waited while the line
clicked and finally rattled.

Polly answered, a strain of cautious anxiety in her voice.

Wager asked for Max, and the anxiety went up half a note. "Yes, Gabe, he's up. I'll get him."

And, a moment later, Max's voice. "Gabe! How you doing out there? Anything helpful?"

He told Max about the avenging angels.

"Mormons? You think the victims have something to do with the Mormons?"

"I don't know, Max. Most of the people here think the drawing means the avenging angels. The one found with Mueller is identical to the one we found."

"Well, it's an approach we haven't tried. There's still no missing persons on either victim. Or identification. The dental charts have been sent around here and in Pueblo, but you know how that goes."

The dental charts were circulated when other means of identification had failed. Usually it went slowly, and sometimes not at all, because response by the dentists was strictly voluntary, and some didn't feel like wasting their time. "Mueller had no known connections with the Mormons or any other church group," Wager told Max. "And the method wasn't the same."

"How's that?"

"He was shot in the back of the head instead of the chest. He wasn't robbed. He was known. He was left in his home."

After a pause Max asked, "So the only real similarity is that sketch?" Then, "What about the slug? Ballistics finally matched the two from Denver and Pueblo—their report came in today: same weapon."

"They can't find a slug." Wager dropped his voice, glad for the brief spurt of radio traffic that drew the girl's ears away from him as she responded to a deputy's query. "The training out here is amateur—almost as bad as the rent-a-cops."

"The sheriff's office doesn't have a detective?"

"Hell, no. The county can't afford one. I don't even know if his deputies are certified."

"Was the trip a waste then?"

Wager didn't know that either. "We found out about these avenging angels. Maybe something will come out of that."

"I hope so . . . but it's a hell of a long drive just for that. Listen, I'll see what I can turn up when I go in tonight. You driving back tomorrow?"

"No reason not to."

"Okay, I'll see you tomorrow night." Max added, "Kolagny's settling for a reduced plea on the barbed-wire killing." His voice masked his disgust; only the fact that he mentioned it told Wager his disappointment.

"What the hell for?"

"He thinks he'll have trouble with intent. The defense is claiming they only wanted to scare Ellison, not kill him."

"They made threats!"

"They claim they didn't." Wager heard a shrug in Max's voice. "It's their word against Linton's, Kolagny says, and he wants a sure thing. What the hell, he's the prosecutor. And a sure thing makes the stats look better. Say, Gabe, can I tell Polly you'll be coming to the barbecue?"

"I—ah—haven't asked Jo yet. I'll ask her when I get back."

"Sure, Gabe. See you tomorrow."

Damn Prosecuting Attorney Kolagny and damn the barbecue. He hung up the telephone and, without seeing, gazed at the closed door of the sheriff's private office. What Max said was true: the only real similarity between Mueller's shooting and those in Denver and Pueblo was the angel drawing. But it was also the only tie they had to anything at all, and even if it made no sense it was better than nothing. Maybe. He hoped it was better than nothing.

At the edge of his hearing the radio popped and Deputy Yates voiced a message for the highway patrol: "I got a 10-50, a pickup rolled into the barrow, mile eighteen, state highway 173. No injuries."

"Ten-four," said the daughter-in-law. "I'll tell him."

Wager waited as she dialed the CHP frequency and relayed the message to a laconic voice somewhere in the dark. Then, the excitement over, she logged the calls and turned back to her *National Enquirer* with a glance at Wager to see if he had noticed how efficient she was.

"Is your husband with the sheriff's office too?"

She nodded. "He's a jailer. We got it fixed so we work the same shifts. No kids yet." She smiled.

If the county commissioners didn't mind the nepotism Wager wasn't going to sweat it. There were few jobs to be had in this corner of the state anyway, and fewer still that brought in any kind of hard cash. Apparently Tice, like everyone else, grabbed for that stray dollar with both hands and with those of all his relatives, and no one thought the worse of him for it. In fact, if he didn't grab, they'd probably think him a damned fool and not worth voting for in the next election.

"Any other relatives working for the sheriff?"

"Sure—his wife fills in here on weekends, and his other boy's the animal control officer." She grew suddenly cautious. "We took a test for it—all the candidates take a test. The highest score gets the job. And all the scores are posted."

Wager believed her; and he had a good idea who wrote the test. "Are all the radio calls logged in?"

Her voice became businesslike. "We try. Sometimes when it gets real busy we have a hard time keeping up. Daryl—Sheriff Tice—tried to get the commissioners to buy a tape recorder. A lot of times the officers will need to know what they radioed in—a name or license number.

But the commissioners said not this year. So we do what we can." Holding up the clipboard, she showed him the mimeographed form with its columns filled with abbreviations under Time, Sender, Message, and Disposition. Most of the entries were in the Uniform Ten-Code and were routine.

When she had talked herself out of her defensive mood, Wager asked what he really wanted to know. "Do you think there are any avenging angels around the county?"

She giggled nervously. "No!" Then she thought a moment. "I mean I didn't—not until I heard about those killings in Denver and Pueblo. And then Mueller got shot. But I don't think I believe in them."

"Are there a lot of people who do?"

"I don't know . . . it's not something you talk about much. Cynthia was scared after Mueller got killed, I know that."

"Who's Cynthia?"

"Cynthia Moreles. She works the day shift."

Wager remembered, "The pretty one?"

"The young one."

"Why's she afraid?"

"I'm not really sure. I just know she heard about Mueller and she just shuddered."

"But she didn't say anything?"

"No. Not to me."

Wager filed the item in his memory; it was a card to be pulled when he got the chance. "Is there a restaurant open this late?"

She glanced at the twenty-four-hour clock, whose hands pointed to 20:00. "The Mesaland restaurant should still be open. They don't close until nine, unless there's no business. Ten on weekends."

Thanking her, Wager headed his Trans-Am toward the steady wink of green-yellow-red in the distance. He found himself driving much more slowly than he did in Denver; there was no place to rush to, and not much to do once he got there. Even the traffic lights seemed to be slower, stopping him for a long time at an empty intersection to look at a gas station closed for the night; at a rambling block of one-story shops with dim lights here and there behind the cluttered windows; at another corner gas station converted into a drive-in curio store, lightless now, and perhaps even out of business judging from the sun-faded signs for real Indian turquoise jewelry.

The Mesaland Motel sat at the west end of town, where the state highway swung south toward the Four Corners region and a main county road aimed west at Utah. Here, where traffic was a bit heavier, there was no light and Wager had to yank his wheel hard to miss a swerving pickup truck that screeched rubber across the highway from the county road. The howl of teenage voices hung in the exhaust behind the weaving truck, the spinning clatter of an empty beer can tossed high in the air, a flashing moment of self-contained noise and excitement and speed challenging the dark indifference of the surrounding night and the silent, vast earth beyond. Wager could remember how, just before going into the Marines, he and his buddies had cruised noisily like those kids. It was as if motion and excitement and laughter could hold back the impending world of adulthood and all its plodding sterility. It had not. In fact, Wager had rushed to meet it, not knowing that the avenue he'd chosen for its excitement and challenge was no different from that of his buddy who went into insurance, or the others who became salesmen or contractors or truck drivers. He shouldn't have joined the Marines at sixteen, but his mother had signed the papers and his sister was glad to see him go. And what the hell, if the old man had been alive he'd have been proud to see his kid in dress blues. Besides, it promised a world where excitement was not only permanent but approved, a world that turned out to be the bleak DMZ in Korea, the orange clay and green jungle of northern Okinawa, the bare crushed coral and barbed wire of Landing Zone Delta in Vietnam. There, not yet twenty-five and already wearing one hashmark, Staff Sergeant Wager saw what he had long suspected: that life was as casual as death, and that the only meaning to be found in either was what he gave to it. Which, he guessed, was what had ultimately landed him in law enforcement when he found himself bored by the kinds of jobs that an infantryman with eight years in the Marine Corps could qualify for. A cop accepted the importance of the rules that tried to order the randomness of life and death, and his job was to go after those who did not accept the rules. Usually they were merely the careless ones; on rare occasions they were the ones who were neither careless nor blind to the rules, but who knew them and chose to stay outside them. That was the real meaning of "outlaw" to Wager, and those were the ones you ruptured yourself to nail, because they were truly dangerous. They reasoned what they did and they struck like feeding sharks at those penned in by the rules; they were the ones who crossed the line between order and chaos, and who brought to their victims not only a fear of death but a terror of the soul.

Nosing the Trans-Am into a vacant slot near the motel's canopied entrance, Wager sat half listening to an adenoidal singing group on the car radio. Those angel drawings had come from that kind of outlaw. He had killed and then left a message, to terrify and to control. To make people run for their lives or shudder with fright. And he had done it, Wager finally admitted to the stillness around and within him, from motives he considered just. He, too, sought justice beyond the law. But Wager saw a difference between himself and the death angel—Tony-O was scum, proven scum that the law couldn't reach but Wager could. The death angel perverted all sense of justice; his reason was founded on madness—it had to be. And when Wager could discover the reason, or the madness, he'd have a clearer idea who'd left the messages and the bodies.

The motel's night clerk was an aggressively friendly and well-scrubbed young man whose smile had not yet become professional. He said, "Sheriff Tice told me you'd be in," handed Wager a key and a card to fill out, and told him that, yes, the kitchen was still open. The dining room was part of the lounge, where a handful of men sat over beers and joked quietly with the big-chested girl behind the bar. Wager ordered trout and a beer from a tired woman who looked like the girl's mother, and leaned against the squeaking plastic of the booth's upright back. It was one of those booths designed to cave in the small of your spine while it pressed against your shoulders, and as Wager squirmed for some kind of comfort a man paused to squint through the dim light.

"You Detective Wager?"

"Yes."

He was broad-shouldered but slim, balding, and had a plaid shirt closed at the neck by a bolo tie with a turquoise slide. The hand he held out was large, with sore-looking knuckles. "Winston—Orrin Winston. I'm the editor of the *Grant County Beacon*. Can I sit down?"

"That's the newspaper?"

"The weekly, not the daily. But we have mostly news that's not fit to print anyway." He sighed as he slid into the facing plastic seat, and lifted the drooping corners of his mouth in a smile. "Like whose dog got hit by a car, or whose cousin came for a visit last weekend. We don't get much in the way of murders or city detectives coming out to investigate. That's real news."

"I'm not here investigating. That's the sheriff's job. I'm just looking for similarities with a homicide we had over in Denver."

"That's another destroying angel killing?"

"I mean a homicide with similarities. That's all."

"Was that other victim a friend or relative of Mueller?"

"The case is still under investigation, Mr. Winston. There's not much I can tell the press about it. You'll have to talk to Sheriff Tice." Wager half wondered if there was some odor about him that lured newspapermen. Manure, perhaps. They liked to gather like flies on any fresh shit they found.

"Oh, sure, I understand. And I'm not going to do a story on you if you don't want it. I'm just trying to do the groundwork for when this thing does break." The drooping mouth lifted and fell again in what was meant to be a friendly way. "This destroying angel thing's a real story, Gabe. I want to claim it before the *Denver Post* or the wires or somebody sends some stringer down here to steal it. You see what I mean?"

"I see. How'd you know about me?"

"This here's a small town. You can't keep many secrets in a town this small. Did you and Yates learn anything new up to Mueller's place? Off the record."

Wager guessed this was the man's way of proving what he said about small towns. "I just looked at the crime scene. Did you know Mueller well?"

"I knew him. Everybody knew him. But nobody knew him well."

"Why?"

"He kept to himself. Worked around for wages when he needed money, and stayed by himself up in his cabin when he didn't." Without being asked, the tired woman brought

Winston a bottle of Coors and he winked "thanks" at her. "See what I mean?" he asked Wager. "Everybody in town knows I drink Coors. Can't sit in any bar in town without getting a Coors shoved at me."

"Do you know any reason why somebody would shoot him?"

Winston shook his head. "Don't know of any man that hated him that much, or any woman that liked him that much."

"What about those avenging angels?"

The head, balding in a wide strip from brow to crown, shook again. "I'm a Mormon—a jack-Mormon, anyway; used to be a Mormon. But I know there's no such thing anymore in the orthodox Mormon church."

"I understand there's different kinds of Mormons around here."

"Well, yes, that's true." Pouring his beer into a tall glass, Winston dropped his voice with a glance toward the waitress. "Some local folks have been kicked out of the Mormon church. Excommunicated, you understand. If anybody around here believed in the destroying angels, it'd be them."

"Why?"

"They claim to be fundamentalist Mormons. They claim the church left the basic teachings and they're the only true Mormons left. They have their own churches and their own prophets."

"Prophets?"

"Sure. The president of the Mormon church is a prophet. If he says God told him Negroes can be saved, then the church lets them in. If he says the MX missile system is against God's will, then the brethren vote against the missiles. If he says God told him polygamy's not to be practiced, then the church won't approve it anymore."

"I get the idea, Mr. Winston."

"Orrin. Just call me Orrin, Gabe." He took a long sip at his beer. "Actually, the church never denied polygamy as a sacred institution revealed by Joe Smith. What happened was they said it was against the laws of the state and its time just hasn't come yet. It was a political maneuver, not a religious one, and a lot of members at that time believed the compromise was a betrayal of the faith."

"At what time? When was this?"

"End of the last century."

Wager blinked. "And people still get excited about that?"

"Well," Winston said mildly, "in generations, that's not too long ago. My own granddaddy was one of them." He started to say something else, but did not.

"You mean you've got local polygamists who still fight the church?"

"And each other. Their fathers were polygamists and their fathers before them. There's maybe four main schisms scattered from here into California and Mexico. Each one claims its own president and prophet. There's some smaller groups, too."

"How do you know so much about them?"

"I was born a Mormon. I've lived here for fifty-five years. I know a lot of people and they talk to me. People who wouldn't give non-Mormons the time of day, they'll ask me if I heard about so-and-so, or do I know what such-and-such did." The square shoulders lifted and fell beneath the plaid shirt. "They're not just being sociable, Gabe. They tell me so they can see something come out in the paper. You get used to it in this business. But if a serious problem does come up and they need the law, they'll tell me and I'll be the one to go to the sheriff with it. That way, nobody out there has broken faith with the brethren and communicated with the Gentiles."

"Gentiles?"

"Non-Mormons. Sometimes they call them strangers or infidels."

"Do they have an ayatollah, too?"

"Ha! I guess it is a little like that. You are either with them or against them, and if you're with them, you do what their prophet says. Some of the groups try to convert the Gentiles, but mostly they try to save other Mormons who follow a different prophet. That's the ones they really go after—false prophets are worse than no prophets at all."

Wager peeled the spine and ribs out of the smoking white flesh of his trout and squeezed lemon juice onto the flaking meat. "And now somebody wants you to tell me something."

Winston leaned back, his shirt rubbing in little squeaks against the plastic. "You catch on fast for a city boy, Gabe."

Some of the Hispanic ways of doing things were just as roundabout as Winston's, but Wager didn't bother explaining. "What are you trying to tell me?"

"How's the fish, Officer? Everything all right?" The waitress stood at the table edge, expecting Wager to say "just fine." When he did, she smiled wearily and said, "You want anything, just holler. Orrin—another beer?"

"In a while, Doris." He waited until she was out of sight again behind the kitchen's swinging doors. "I didn't tell her you were an officer." The baggy lips smiled. Then, when Wager didn't answer, Winston went on. "They want to know who got shot over in Denver and Pueblo."

"Who's 'they'?"

Winston shook his head. "I'm not supposed to tell you that. They won't like me saying this much."

"How'd they know about the Pueblo killing?"

"That flyer from over there that came into the sheriff's office a couple weeks ago. Then yours came in just behind it. Both had the destroying angel drawings."

"But how in hell did civilians learn about that?"

"How did Doris know you're a policeman?"

"From the kid at the front desk. Mr. Winston, I'm not here to talk about cases that are under investigation. If 'they' have information, they should tell Tice. If they want information, then they should ask Tice. Or call the Denver Police Department and talk to Chief Doyle. He's the only one to authorize information." That wasn't quite true, but sometimes the bureaucracy could be used in this kind of game.

Winston rubbed an arthritic hand along the strip of scalp. "Those queries of yours weren't marked confidential. In fact, Sheriff Tice showed me the Pueblo letter and asked me if I knew anything about it, because he knew what the destroying angel meant." Winston sipped and took a different approach. "Look, Detective Wager—Gabe—say a man has two, three, maybe four wives, and maybe ten or fifteen kids. In the eyes of the law, only one family is legal; the others are bastards—no legal rights at all. And the man can go to jail for bigamy and leave those people to starve. It's happened."

"I'm only interested in avenging angels."

"But these people don't know that. You're the law. With Tice," Winston shrugged, "they have a kind of understanding, and the Mormon vote keeps him in office. But you're an outside lawman, and the law's been after these people for a hundred years."

"I'm out of my jurisdiction, Winston. I'm no more law than any other citizen in this county." That, too, wasn't quite true, except for the polygamists. "Now suppose you tell me why two people killed in Denver and Pueblo are so important to somebody around here."

It took Winston a long silence and a quick half-glass of beer before he could get started. "Well, take those ten or fifteen kids. A man might have some of them work his ranch. Others he'd send out to work to bring in hard cash to the family. Or tribe. I think of them as a tribe. Anyway, a lot of people working here in town are related in some way to the people on the benchland, and even if that blood gets sort of mixed up sometimes, it's still thicker than water. A lot of these people call each other cousin, but they're not. They're half-brother or half-sister. Same pa, just a different wife. Even if they don't see each other much, the ties are still there; and when trouble comes to one, it can pull in a whole raft of cousins."

No wonder the Mormons were so interested in genealogy. "What about you? Do you have any of these cousins?"

Winston looked at him for a long minute, and then nodded once. "My pa had three wives. My ma was the middle one. I got four real brothers and sisters, and twelve more I call cousin. That old sonofabitch Pa, he lived to be eighty-three and died courting a fourth wife. I can't spit in a high wind around this county without hitting a relative of one kind or another. I got a lot of kin over on the benchland. That's why they talk to me, despite the fact I don't claim their brand of Mormonism." He added, "I'm not a believer in polygamy, Gabe; I saw what kind of life Ma got out of it. But some of Pa's kids think there's nothing wrong with it because that was the way they were raised."

Wager stared at the man's level, dark eyes, feeling some weird shift of time that made him wonder if he was really sitting here in the last quarter of the twentieth century. From the corner jukebox a pinched voice wailed a country-and-western ballad about somebody not loving somebody anymore; the rumble of slow voices at the bar was punctuated by the sharp *tink* of bottle on glass; from behind the kitchen door came the raised voices of the crew closing down the stoves and cleaning up. Formica table, plastic seats, imitation wooden columns hinting at a division between eating area and lounge. All modern and forgettable. And this man telling Wager things that suddenly made real and immediate the stories that earlier had sounded as if they had been old a hundred years ago. "You're married?"

"One wife."

The modern way was to have your wives in sequence; the old was to have them all at the same time. Fifty years ago, the sequential way was called a sin; fifty years from now, polygamy might not be. "Well," Wager said, "you tell whatever cousin asked you that we don't know who was killed. We haven't been able to identify either victim."

"No idea at all? You're sure?"

"I'm not lying to you, Winston."

"Take it easy, Gabe—I didn't mean that the way it sounded. I'm just anxious to know, that's all."

"We have no missing-persons calls that match the victims. No fingerprint identification. No dental records. Nothing. If your cousins know of someone who's missing, they should tell me. Without an i.d. of the victims, we don't have much chance to catch the killers."

"I see." Winston poured more pale beer into his glass and rubbed a finger around the rim to oil it, letting the foam rise high above the glass before he bobbed his head to sip at it. "The fact you have no records on the victims . . ." He wagged his head once, and then explained. "These people have to live outside the law, Gabe; they don't register for the draft or join social security. They can't go to the police when they have trouble. They want nothing to do with a government that they see as an enemy."

"Who do they think the victims are?"

"Do you have any photographs of the two?"

"Is someone missing from around here?"

"I don't know, Gabe! They tell me what they want me to know, and that's all. But they know each other and they keep in touch. Even if one part of the church lives across the state, they visit a lot and they write."

"How many people are in these churches?"

"In my, ah, cousin's church, he's got maybe four or five hundred scattered over Utah and Arizona."

"That many?"

Winston shrugged. "There's a church along the southern Arizona line that claims a couple thousand in the U.S. and Mexico."

Wager pulled the brown envelope from his vest pocket and slid out two of the i.d. photographs. They had been touched up by the police artist to approximate what the victims must have looked like when alive. "You recognize them?"

Winston's scalp gleamed in the dim light as he shook his head slowly. "If you'll let me, I'd like to show them around."

"Around where?"

"The benchland."

"Sure. As long as I come with you."

5.

By the time Winston picked him up the next morning the newsman was resigned to Wager's going along. Something had made him agree to Wager's shaky argument that the photos were classified documents in an ongoing investigation and that any unauthorized use of them was punishable by fine or imprisonment or both. It had sounded good last night after a few beers, but today he wondered if the newsman had really been fooled. Something was going on —Wager wasn't too dumb to see that; even if he didn't yet know what lay behind Winston's carefully chosen words or his occasional thoughtful silences, it was clear that Winston wasn't showing all his cards. It was a bit like fishing: a gentle, slow approach, a delicate twitch of the rod to give the lure its lifelike motion on the still water, a lot of patience. The way, Wager thought wryly, he should have approached Cynthia Moreles.

The sheriff's young clerk had been at her desk when Wager arrived a little after eight, following a motel breakfast of huevos rancheros and a wad of greasy hash-brown potatoes that kept exploding in his stomach with gaseous regularity. When she smiled good morning he nodded and asked if he could talk to her for a few minutes.

"Me? Sure, I guess. What for?"

"I'd like some information about the avenging angels."

Her lipstick stood out against the sudden paleness of her face and she almost pushed back against the desk. But she said nothing.

"Do you believe in them, Cynthia?"

Her glance went to the woman at the radio console, across to Tice's door, to the busy blond, and then back to Wager in a plea. "I don't even want to talk about them. Please."

"Have they ever threatened you?"

"No," she murmured. "Please." She turned quickly to busy herself with a stack of warrants, keeping her face down until Wager finally wandered over to his own corner of the office and sat and waited for Winston. Avoiding his eyes, she managed to find all her work on the other side of the room; and Wager, glad to get away from the bruised feelings that radiated from the girl, gave up and went outside to wait.

Orrin Winston arrived more or less when he said he would in a Dodge pickup truck carrying a CB antenna and a sun-faded magnetic sign on the door: GRANT COUNTY BEACON. "Morning, Gabe. Let's take my truck. They see that thing of yours, and they won't even answer the door. Besides, you'd leave your transmission hung up on some rock halfway there."

Wager had noticed the bent rear license plates on many of the local cars. In Denver that was done to hide the number from police eyes; here, it was from dragging on steep dirt roads.

"You got those confidential pictures with you?" Winston

wore a different plaid shirt but the same bolo tie with its turquoise stone like an oily fragment of the sky. A sweat-stained Stetson shaded his balding scalp.

"I brought them."

It was all they said for the next five or ten miles; only the occasional twanging jabber of the CB broke the silence. Finally Wager asked about what had been troubling him all morning. "Do you know of any recent threats or assaults around here by the avenging angels?"

Winston thought, before saying with a shrug, "Not recent. Not for years. Like I told you last night, Gabe, I really don't think they're around here anymore."

"Not even since Mueller?"

His head wagged once. "You got me there. But if it was an angel, he must have been from outside—Denver, maybe. Where you found the other one. But damn it, there's no reason to kill Mueller—Danite or not."

"Danite?"

"Sons of Dan. That's what the Mormons call the destroying angels." He shook his head. "I'd swear Mueller had nothing to do with any Mormons around here. And he didn't have a damn thing anybody could want. No money. And that ranch of his isn't worth spit." His head shook again. "Unless my cousin knows something about it that he hasn't told me, I can't see any connection at all between Mueller and anybody, let alone a Mormon sect."

"What about other local people? I talked to somebody who was too scared to say a word about the avenging angels."

"Oh?" He geared down for a cattle guard, beyond which the county highway narrowed to a roughly patched strip of tar that jolted the white pickup and made something clatter rhythmically beneath Wager's feet. "Well, some people are still afraid of them, that's true. Personally, I think it's like being afraid of ghosts, but there's a lot of people believe in ghosts, too. Who'd you talk to?"

Wager wondered how much to tell this lean man he had met just last night, and who seemed so open and friendly. But the girl made no secret of being afraid. She couldn't keep a fear like that hidden. "Cynthia Moreles."

"Ah—well, yeah." Winston's sagging mouth widened briefly, but it was not in a smile. "If anybody's got reason I guess she has, poor thing."

"Why's that?"

"They killed her granddaddy. Lord, over twenty years ago now."

"The avenging angels did?"

"That's what people said. But nothing was ever proven and nobody was ever caught. The sheriff—the one before Tice—didn't try too damned hard. That's how Tice got the job: beat him out on just that killing." Winston said "um" and added, "Cynthia was maybe three or four years old, but I guess she remembers the whole thing. Terrified the poor girl, and I guess she'll never get over it."

"What made people think it was the avenging angels?"

"There wasn't any picture, if that's what you're thinking." He tipped his Stetson back. "The Moreles family, they've been here since God knows when. Before the first Mormons, anyway. The Mexicans pushed out the Indians, and the Mormons pushed out the Mexicans. Cynthia's granddaddy—Ramon Maria Moreles—he fought in a local Mormon war when he was a teenager. Maybe 1893–94. Their family lost it and it cost them a lot of land—good land, too. Land, water rights, everything. But old Ramon, he never gave up, and the older he got the louder he got against Mormons of all stripes. About that time—the sixties and all—some Mexicans down in New Mexico started looking up old land grants and suing in court for property they claimed had been stolen from them a hundred years ago. Ramon started doing the same thing here. I tell you, he really stirred things up. Hell, he might have been on to something, too; he had enough to get a couple lawyers interested, anyway. Then three men broke in one night and shot him."

"But they didn't say they were avenging angels?"

"No, they didn't. But everybody in the county knew what the motive was, and the Mormons were settled on that contested land. Ramon made no secret about what he wanted to do—he was a little bit crazy on the subject, you understand. And besides, he was a Catholic." Winston added, "The Pope's a rival prophet, you see."

"I've heard."

"Well, the belief was that the local Mormons really felt threatened, so they called in some cousins or whatever from Utah to settle Ramon's claim permanently."

"And Cynthia's still afraid?"

"She was there. I did the story on it, and she was one of the witnesses. Three masked men kicked open the door, shot the old man, and drove off, just like that." A series of jolts rattled the truck. "The land case never did go to court; no Moreles has mentioned land grants or Mormons since. Not loud enough to be heard, anyway. But I can't blame Cynthia for being afraid. The Moreles claim could still go to court."

Wager stared out the window at the surrounding land. It had gradually dried out, and the grassy meadows near town were replaced by a carpet of lumpy, gray-green sagebrush. Here and there a Hereford lifted a white face with dull pink eyes toward the sound of the truck. What Winston had told him could explain the girl's fear. Cynthia was somewhere in her midtwenties, and a memory like that, reinforced by the wailing family, the funeral, the police, and officials and reporters—all speaking English—

it would be bitter and long lasting. "Was any of that property near Mueller's?"

"No," said Winston. "Good try, but it was all down here. We just crossed over some of it."

The dry rangeland glided past the quivering glass of the truck's window. "This isn't open range?"

"It is now. BLM land—Bureau of Land Management— since we crossed that cattle guard. The ranchers lease it for their cows." He turned the truck onto a dirt road marked only by a Stop sign. It led straight west for a mile or two and then, without warning, tilted sharply down in a sequence of switchbacks. Winston halted the truck at the edge, and Wager felt as if they were at the bow of a gigantic ship that nosed into a stiffened sea of stepped and falling waves. In a series of giant benches, the plateau they stood on dropped away, gradually leaving behind the clusters and dots of juniper, the clinging sage and cactus, and becoming almost totally naked sand and wind-polished rock. Past each shelf of land, troughs of red and purple led to deeper troughs, which dropped out of sight. Rising from unglimpsed depths, flat-topped mountains and spires of rock and mesa seemed poised to fall. After turning off the engine, they got out to stand in the hot wind that rose steadily from the treeless rock and sand below. Its sough was as vast as the space it scoured, and was deepened by the distant shrill scream of a hawk gliding along one of the faces of rock below.

"The benchland."

Winston spoke with awe, as if he had said "the promised land" or "the magic land," and Wager wondered just how far the newsman really was from his Mormon past. "Is this where you were raised?"

"Born and raised. Over in that canyon—Green Water Canyon." He pointed to a large notch that twisted between two mesas painted red and orange and white in the morning sun. The bottom of the canyon was out of sight, its lower reaches dim with the haze of distance and the shadows of massive walls. "That's forty-five miles away, line of sight. Over a hundred on the ground."

And, Wager thought as they climbed back into the truck, maybe a century or two in time. If time meant anything out here

The switchbacks led sharply down the escarpment to drop into the shadow etched across benches and slopes. Despite the shade of the east rim, the dry air warmed the cab and both men lowered their windows. A low streak of dust twenty miles away marked the passage of some other vehicle, but that was the only motion besides their own that Wager could see in the hundred miles of broken horizon. He recalled reading somewhere about the upheaval of these mountains now out of sight behind them, the newest version of the Rocky Mountains. Here, they must have lifted out of some shallow sea, sending oceans of churning, carving waters through layers of sandstone shelves and loose sediment, knifing first a fissure, then a gully, then a canyon as the fall of water became steeper and its grit abraded faster and deeper through the colored rock: red from iron oxide, the black of lava ash, pale yellows of bleached ocean sands, the thin green of copper or sulphur ash. What streams remained now twisted their way to join the Colorado, their muddy, boiling water draining from the snows of the mountains behind. Here and there they dammed a lake, whose own gigantic size was dwarfed by the spread of empty rock and vacant sky. Then the water once more became a thin vein, sheltered from the thirsty sun by towering cliffs, and rushing to reach the Gulf of California before it disappeared into the dry air or hungry sands.

"This here's an arm of Escalante Canyon." Their road

ran straight out on a nose formed by one of the benches, then branched off into more steep switchbacks. "That way takes you over to Lake Powell and the Indian reservations." He pointed to a purple notch on the horizon. "This way's the road toward Green River—except you can't get all the way there by car. We'll get to the bottom pretty soon."

But by the time the dirt track finally leveled out, Wager felt himself numbed by the glare of sun bouncing off the tilted rock surrounding him, the ceaseless rush of hot wind, the endless shifting of canyon walls that slowly drew closer to the road. Even the swirl of dust devils spinning across the dotted waste failed to startle him awake anymore. Dulled by the heat and the motion, eyes heavy from squinting against the sun, he felt suspended, as if he were a fixed point, and the rock and sand and glare swung and jolted past him.

Winston turned off the larger track onto a two-rut lane that occasionally disappeared entirely as it wound upward and through a saddle between steep red cliffs, then down again over lurching wind-polished slabs of rock. "Here we are."

Ahead, like a mirage, Wager saw a startling swath of green ridged by irrigation ditches. A line of flickering Lombardy poplars ran beside the main ditch leading from the river into the maze of field branches. At one end of the clearing, masked by the sun-blanched green of willows and the taller, restless leaves of cottonwoods, a collection of buildings and sheds and pens sprawled in the shade.

"It looks deserted."

"They know we're coming—we raised plenty of dust coming through the notch." He added, "I hope he ties up them damn dogs."

Gradually the trees revealed a two-story square house sitting like a carved block of stone in the deep shade. As they approached, a single figure walked slowly into the whiteness of sunlight and stood motionless for the ten minutes it took the truck to wind down the wall and across the rough canyon floor. When they finally pulled up to the man in a swirl of pink dust and clatter, he nodded once, wide straw hat bobbing down and up briefly, and said, "Orrin."

The newsman nodded just as curtly. "This here's Gabe Wager. He's a lawman from Denver, Zenas. I brought him because I trust him. You can too. He's got some pictures. Gabe, Zenas Winston."

The fully bearded man did not offer to shake hands. Like Orrin, he was slender but broad-shouldered, and there was some similarity in the nose and especially the dark eyes. Wager couldn't see much of his mouth or chin beneath the squared-off beard.

"All right, then; come on in." He turned abruptly and raised his voice to the unseen but noisily wailing dogs, "You, Pious! You, Leo! Hush up!"

They followed the man's work-stiff stride into the shade of the trees, where the weight of sun suddenly lifted. Wager caught glimpses of towheaded children peeking like animals hiding from a predator behind outbuildings or screens of willows. The sound of the shallow river blended with the rustle of cottonwood leaves, and somewhere behind the outbuildings a bird whistled persistently above the flat clank of an animal's bell. Zenas led them to the farmhouse. Its mortarless walls were of brown sandstone, its windows and doors framed in thick wooden timbers that had faded almost to white. The concrete entry slab was patterned with brightly colored stones set in some kind of awkward script that Wager couldn't make out. Upstairs, a baby cried fitfully, and Wager had the feeling that the life of the house had drawn back to watch and listen invisibly until the strangers were gone. The parlor was a small room, sparsely furnished with a dark shiny table and a few overstuffed chairs that Wager's ex-wife would have called "antique Victorian." One wall was hung with photographs, the top rows having the brown, stiff look of tintypes; the bottom ones were stiff, too, but in a more modern way, as if both subject and photographer knew the picture would go on that wall. Wager did not think he saw Orrin's face among the generally young men and women who peered back. A dark oak chest of drawers filled another wall, and closed doors led to the rest of the house. Wager suspected that this was a room for meditation or prayer, or formal counsels. Zenas, taking off his straw cowboy hat to show his own strip of balding scalp, pointed a work-thickened finger at the chairs. "Be comfortable." He waited until Orrin and Wager sat, then he sat himself in the largest of the chairs, the only one with arms. As soon as he was settled, one of the white doors opened and a woman wordlessly brought in a large pitcher and three glasses. She filled them silently, serving first Wager, then Orrin, and finally Zenas, who was equally quiet until she disappeared, her ankle-length dress whispering across the frame as the door closed behind her.

"Ease your thirst."

Wager was not certain whether Zenas was used to giving orders or unused to showing manners to infidels. Probably a little of both, plus a strong sense of the patriarchal dignity needed to govern his tribe. He was certain that the man was not acting this way to impress Wager; what a stray Gentile might think would never trouble Zenas's mind.

When the glasses of cool, tart apple juice were emptied, the man gazed at Orrin. "Well?"

"He don't know the names of the two, so he's brought some pictures to show you."

The dark eyes turned to Wager, who held the photographs out to Zenas. The man carefully studied first one face and then the other until, without a sound, he rose and went into another room, shutting the door behind him.

"He's gone to show them to Miriam. She's the one who brought in the drink."

"Which wife's she?" murmured Wager.

"First. That's why she served the drink."

"The tribe of Zenas."

"Lo, they wandered in the desert until the Lord delivered them unto Zion."

"And showed them the way of the righteous."

"The way of the self-righteous." Orrin winked.

When Zenas came back he handed the pictures to Wager and sat and stared at the wall of photographs.

Wager gave him a few minutes. He heard footsteps somewhere on the second floor. The baby's cry had stopped abruptly with the muffled sound of feeding, but a young voice drifted through the curtained window, earnestly talking about something indecipherable. A bird whistled. Wager raised an eyebrow at Orrin, who gave a slight shake of his head and sat still. Finally Zenas sighed, as if waking from a light sleep.

"We know them. Both of them. They are brethren of the church."

"Names?" said Wager. "Can you give me names, Mr. Winston?"

"I can. This one is Asa Kruse." The thick finger moved to the face of the man found in Denver. "This one is Ervil Beauchamp."

When Zenas said nothing more, Wager asked, "Can you tell me why somebody would shoot them?"

Zenas, looking at Orrin rather than at Wager, said bitterly, "They were killed by the Antichrist!"

Again Wager waited, until finally he had to ask, "What's that mean?"

"Tell him, Zenas," said Orrin. "You can trust him."

The beard wagged once, in either agreement or resignation. Then he began to speak in a kind of biblical cadence. "There were two brothers, Ervil and Willis Beauchamp, sons of Jonathan Beauchamp, who saw that the Salt Lake people had turned from God's commandments, and followed a false prophet, and refused to return to the ways of the Lord. So Jonathan Beauchamp gathered up his people and fled. He fled first into Arizona to Short Creek, where he lived in peace until the Lord saw fit to visit punishment upon his people by sending the Gentile police down on them. Once more he fled, going down into Mexico, where the Lord saw fit to gather up Jonathan. Before he died, the progenitor anointed the head of Ervil, naming him President of the High Priesthood. Then the sons of Jonathan settled their wives and chattels in Mexico. There, after much travail, the Lord rewarded them for their faithfulness to his Word and they prospered, for what the Lord taketh he returneth a hundredfold to the faithful. But the enemy of the faithful never sleeps." A callused finger rose in warning.

Wager listened to the man recount the religious history of an obscure handful of fanatics in the only formal language he knew, and he found nothing at all to laugh at.

"Dissension came between the brothers, and Willis, the younger, claimed to be Prophet, Seer, and Revelator. Ervil spoke against this false claim, and their people divided into a true and a false church and warred among themselves. And it brought down the armies of the papists who, like the armies of the pharaohs of old, only awaited their chance to move against the children of righteousness whose lands they coveted. And Willis, listening to the

Enemy of God, did denounce his brother, Ervil, and join with the papists to drive them from their homes and scatter Ervil and his followers to wander without rest in the lands of strangers."

Orrin sat up suddenly, eyes wide. "Is that who came here, what, two or three years ago?"

"He and some of his people came asking help, and the Lord moved my heart to charity."

"Where did they go from here?" asked Wager.

Zenas still spoke to Orrin, as if the story had to be filtered first through half-faithful ears. "They went to hide among the Gentiles, abiding the Lord's time until Ervil could gird up his loins to strike back at Willis and destroy this false brother and false prophet."

"But where?" Wager insisted. "What was his last address?"

"Zenas, it's the only way. Already those two are dead. And Mueller, too."

"Mueller is a Gentile. He's not important dead or alive."

"But not Asa or Ervil," Orrin said. "And their families —you know what the destroying angel means."

The bearded man closed his eyes for a long moment, as if asking once more for strength or guidance from some inner voice. When he opened them, he looked directly at Wager. "West Mosier Street—2444."

"In Denver? The Mosier Street in Denver?"

"Even so."

The long, bumpy climb back was hot, and the wind carried the dust into the cab to coat Wager's teeth with a gritty film and to make his watering eyes itch. Tears dried at their corners, making them crusty, and he felt the sweat glue his back to the jiggling, thumping seat behind him.

"Do you think he doesn't know Mueller?"

"He said Mueller was a Gentile. He wants nothing to do with Gentiles, alive or dead. Zenas wouldn't lie, Gabe; if he or one of his church members had killed Mueller, he'd tell you. Kruse and Beauchamp are important to him, but Mueller's not."

"Why did he come to you about those two?"

"You mean did he expect to know them? I'm not sure, Gabe. When Tice showed me the angel drawings from the Denver and Pueblo killings, I drove out and asked Zenas about them. Maybe he guessed it was them—he knew Beauchamp was in Denver. Certainly any mention of Danites is enough to make him curious." The man reached inside his flannel shirt and scratched somewhere on his bony chest. "Zenas isn't going to tell everything he knows, not to me, anyway. But both men had families—big ones —and the destroying angels are angels of death to all their enemies."

"He could have written Beauchamp's family. He had their address, and he could have written to find out if it was Beauchamp without ever talking to you."

Winston tipped his hat back off his forehead. The gleam of sweat dried quickly in the hot air. "Maybe he did, and got no answer. Or maybe he didn't want any letters leading from Beauchamp to him. I think Zenas is afraid."

"He doesn't seem to be the type."

"Not for himself—for his family and his church. He sheltered Ervil, and he belongs to the same sect as Ervil. I think Ervil ordained Zenas as a High Priest of Melchizedek. That makes Zenas an enemy. And all his people."

"Melchizedek?"

"The immediate ordination by Jesus Christ himself. Just like he laid hands on Saint Peter and ordained him."

"Aw, come on!"

"True, Gabe. Joe Smith claimed a vision that told him to

restore that priesthood. Your orthodox Mormons have the same thing, but of course they don't recognize Zenas's ordination. Which is only fair," he added, "since he doesn't recognize theirs." Orrin glanced at Wager. "Zenas isn't crazy, Gabe. I think he's one of the sanest men I know, and absolutely dedicated to the welfare of his family and church—spiritual and physical. He just believes different things, that's all. His values are of his faith, not his bankbook. There's that statue of Brigham Young built by the church in Salt Lake City—Zenas says the orthodox church placed it with Brigham's backside to the Temple and his hands out to the bank, and that's a sign from God how wrong they've become and how right he is."

Wager remembered how, as Orrin's truck backed in a turn from the ranch, a giggling boy with bare feet and sun-white hair ran from a toolshed to jump into his father's arms. Zenas lifted the boy high, swung him grinning across the sky, then wrapped him in both arms and nuzzled his rough beard against the boy's ticklish neck. Their laughter carried clearly over the straining clatter of the truck.

Watching the two show their love for each other, and seeing the isolated ranch and its shelter of trees and rock, Wager realized how, with only a slight shift of assumptions, all that Zenas believed could seem normal. And he realized, too, that if avenging angels did come after them, they could drop down through the narrow gullies and crevices, suddenly raid and slaughter without discovery, and fade back into the desert canyons. No one would find the victims for weeks or even months. All in the name of God's love.

"Lord, what a story," said Winston half aloud. "I don't know how much of it the cousins will let me use, but what a story when it finally breaks!"

"Why would they hide in Denver and Pueblo?" Wager waved a hand at the serried and hazy shadows that, with the sun moving behind them, had grown mysteriously dark and far away and almost cold. "Why wouldn't they hide out here?"

"That desert's home to all of them. It's the first place Willis would look, and he knows that country. But a quiet house in a city surrounded by people who look no different from them . . . Camouflage, isn't that what they call it?"

Wager nodded, his mind still on the man behind them and the involved web of relationships revealed by Zenas and Orrin. "Is he a younger 'cousin' of yours?"

"Yeah," said Orrin. "The youngest of all. They say that's what really killed Pa—he ran out of the alphabet with Zenas."

b.

When Wager finally eased the Trans-Am into the parking slot behind his Denver apartment, the ten o'clock news was on the car radio. He sat, half listening, and rubbed his fingers across his burning eyes before hauling the overnight bag out of the back seat. The news headlines were tiresomely familiar—wars and rumors of wars, homicides attempted and completed, prices rising and quality falling. He suspected he could have written the headlines before he left for the Western Slope and then simply filled in the names of people or places when he got back. Clicking off the radio, he rode in the stuffy elevator up to his apartment and spent the next five minutes opening windows and doors and chasing out air pent up for the last three days and even staler in contrast to that of the Western Slope. The answering machine sat cold and dark, no messages, but the little pile of mail wedged into the box in the lobby was full of letters trying to sell him things he didn't want or asking for money for the things he shouldn't have bought. One folded slip of paper had neither stamp nor address, just a hastily scrawled "Welcome back—J."

He glanced at his watch; a bit late to try, but what the hell. He dialed Jo's number anyway and let it ring more than the usual six times. Maybe over at her mother's; a date, maybe. It wasn't as if he owned her or asked her not to date anyone else. But he couldn't help that little empty feeling as he hung up the phone and stood for a few minutes in the cool air of the balcony and listened to the rush of traffic below, a wet sound that was strangely harsh to ears that had listened to silence for the last three days. As he gazed down at the swirling lights and wondered if she was at her mother's, it came to him that when he was mulling over all those half-formed ideas for retirement or getting the hell out of Denver, not once had he included Jo in those thoughts. As predictably as the radio news or the standard offense form, his thoughts had been peopled only by himself; perhaps it was best that way—best for her certainly, and perhaps for him, too. When isolation became that comfortable—that reflexive—perhaps it was best not to try to break it.

Rummaging through the refrigerator for a frozen dinner that would not make demands on time or taste, he slid it in the oven and then stood for a long time under the pummeling needles of a hot shower. What he really wanted was sleep, but he went on duty in less than two hours. A shower and shave would have to do instead. What the hell, it wasn't the first time.

He arrived at the division offices just before midnight. Munn belched and asked sourly, "You had some time off?"

"Special assignment. Anything going?"

"Same old shit." He tossed a list of addresses to Wager, locations where statistics said crimes were likely and patrols—marked and unmarked—were to be increased. "Had an officer shot at over near Bayoud and Raritan. No suspects. I don't know what Max has got. He never gets here early." Another belch. "Golding's my partner on this shift. He's out eating supper, for Christ's sake. Mexican food. I wish to hell I had a special assignment to get me away from this goddamn place."

"Take the rest of the day off."

"Big deal—ten minutes." But his hand was already pulling the door closed as he said it.

Wager poured the watch's first cup of coffee from the stained Silex and settled to his desk and its stack of unopened mail. Most of it was junk, a different version of the crap that came to his apartment. But, like idle conversation used to pass the hours of a boring tour of duty, most of the pieces of paper asked conventional questions and called for conventional answers. He threw away the ads for a new kind of quick-release holster manufactured by a Hollywood supply company, for the Brotherhood of Peace Officers insurance package, for a complete set of study manuals with practice examinations for all grades of law enforcement. He tried to concentrate on the requests for information concerning this or that missing person described as "last seen wearing"—sometimes they turned up in the morgue. Mostly juveniles, male and female, though there seemed to be an increasing number of middle-aged women. Statistics would come out with that discovery one of these days and send a circular around on it. Half a dozen other notices on unsolved homicides, with their characteristics. But no more angels. FBI alerts to the following armed and dangerous criminals believed to be approaching or in your vicinity. Memos on procedure changes, saturation areas, special directions for the uniformed watch that plain clothes should be alerted to . . . Wager made a strong effort to focus his attention, but even as he stared at the familiar papers and their familiar phrases, he felt a ludicrous sense of the distance between himself sitting here and himself this afternoon sitting in Winston's truck as it labored up the steep walls of the benchland. It did not seem possible that such divergent geographies and times could be within hours of each other; that this, the electronic world of Denver, was unfelt by those on the other side of the mountains. But why not? Winston and all his cousins had existed over there for a long time, and Wager had never heard of them, either. Would still exist unperceived, except for the avenging angels. It was as if time had moved at a different speed for them. But was their life really that different? Wager, sitting here surrounded by the mechanically printed data of electronic surveillance and retrieval, the automatic copies of in-house communications, the glowing screens and print-outs of "processed" words, was still dealing with the same timeless fears and hatreds that were found on both sides of those mountains. The deeper currents of life were the same in all places and all times; and, in one guise or another, avenging angels were with us always. The trick was to catch them.

"Evening, Gabe." Max, his own memos and notices a small wad in his fist, greeted Wager as always. "Good trip?" And at Wager's nod, "I went around to most of the Mormon churches. Nobody recognized those two John Does."

"I'm not surprised." He waited until Max was seated at his desk and leafing through papers before adding, "But I got positive i.d.'s and a local address."

"What?"

He said it again.

"Jesus, Gabe, why didn't you call it in?"

"I wasn't near a phone until late this afternoon, and I was on my way back anyhow."

Max's eyes narrowed. "What time did you get in?"

"Couple hours ago."

The large head wagged once, a mixture of wonder and

resignation. There was no sense trying to coax Wager to take the day off; Max had seen him do this too many times and knew what the answer would be. Still, he couldn't help hinting: "There's not a damn thing new since you've been gone. A couple weapons fired; no deaths. There's nothing I can't handle by myself."

Wager tossed another handful of paper into the trash. "I'm all right."

Max sighed. "Okay. So who are the victims, and why the angels?"

When Wager finished, Max gave that mostly silent whistle between his teeth that told Wager he was turning each fact over and fitting the pieces against one another in different ways. "You went by the Beauchamp address already." It wasn't a question.

"Yes. No answer. No lights."

"Yeah—they probably ran as soon as they read Beauchamp's description in the papers." Then, "That explains why we have no missing persons on him. They were too afraid to even claim the body."

"And no government records of any kind. They don't join anything," said Wager.

The little whistle. "It's a closed subculture, isn't it? It shares space with the dominant culture, but it doesn't live off it, and it doesn't mix with it. It's actually invisible."

Wager shifted uncomfortably; once in a while, Max slipped into that college sociology bullshit. "Except when they kill somebody."

"Right. The one they found in Loma Vista, he's part of this same group?"

"Mueller. I don't think so. I can't figure how he ties to Beauchamp. Not yet, anyway."

"Maybe he knew something. Or saw someone."

That was possible, and Wager had already thought of it.

But those were just two more of a number of possibilities at that end of the case, and none of them seemed to pull the facts together. Wager drained his cup and drew out the manila file labeled John Doe #17. He rummaged through the tangle of forms and slips and paper clips in his desk drawer for a roll of gummed labels. When he was finished, the folder read "Beauchamp, Ervil" and held a half-page synopsis of what Wager had found out so far. He wedged it back into the full tray of active cases and slid the drawer shut. For the rest of the night, Wager and Max would deal with the kind of violence they were at home with: the logical insanity of East Colfax and Capitol Hill. Tomorrow he could focus on the more exotic kind, which had splashed over from Loma Vista.

In the morning light the Beauchamp house looked as empty as it had last night. Wager, unsuccessfully fighting off a yawn that made his jaw crack, spent a few seconds looking at the house before knocking once more at the door. It was, like its neighbors, a tract house with the look of the late '50s—square, small entry porch centered in a wall of Masonite siding, one story with a low roof of asphalt shingles, full basement, whose windows peeped above metal wells along the foundation. A patched sidewalk evenly divided the small square of lawn, which was shaggy and brown in spots. At each side, he could glimpse a chain-link fence, masked by tall lilac bushes, which sealed off the backyard. The curtains, drawn across the picture window, didn't move, and no one answered his knock.

He walked around to the fence and peered through the lilac leaves into the backyard. There the grass was worn to gray dirt by traffic, and a well-used swing set hung idle among a brightly colored scattering of toy trucks and plastic shovels and pails. No sound came from the large yard or the house.

It was six of one and half a dozen of the other; Wager's mental coin came down tails and he headed for the house on the left. A woman in her midtwenties, with brown eyes and cropped, bleached hair, half opened the door. If Wager had not been so tired he might have been a little more subtle; the Bulldog liked his officers to speak softly and carry a low profile when dealing with Joan Q. Public. But Wager's baggy eyes felt as bristly as his unshaven jaw, and the wariness in the woman's expression as she faced this scruffy figure led his hand to his badge case. "Detective Wager, ma'am. Denver Police. I'd like to ask you some questions about the folks next door."

Her name was Cheryl Johnson and she hadn't seen anybody at the Wilsons' house for—oh, at least a week now. Not that she knows them that well—they seemed to stay pretty much to themselves ever since they moved in almost a year back. Renters. They don't own the house, she knows that, because it had been for sale for a long time before a real estate agency finally bought it and put up a rental sign and the Wilsons came just after that. She's sure they got it pretty cheap and she's often wondered if that wasn't the best way—rent instead of buy. You don't build up equity, but you don't have all the worry about taxes and upkeep, either, and if you're just starting out and don't intend to stay in a neighborhood anyway . . .

"Yes, ma'am. Can you tell me anything about the Wilsons?"

Well they always have a whole houseful of people, she knows that, and she has no idea where everybody sleeps. They have relatives visiting all the time—Mrs. Wilson's two sisters and all their kids. A half-dozen of all ages, but they are real nice and polite, even if they didn't join the neighborhood walkathon for the March of Dimes. They take real good care of the house, which a lot of renters don't do. Her kids play with them sometimes, but the Wilsons never leave their yard. Shy—except when they think no one is looking, and then they have their share of fussing and fighting just like everybody else. The oldest Wilson girl baby-sits and she's real good with kids and real friendly. But she never talks much about herself—you can ask all sorts of questions and she'll just nod or smile and never give you a straight answer. Shy. And she seems kind of—well—out of touch. Like the way she admires Mrs. Johnson's dresses and shoes, which aren't all that stylish; not dowdy, you know, but good quality, and good gracious the cost of clothes these days, and most of them not worth half what you pay for them. Anyway, Naomi Wilson, that's the girl's name, is real good with kids, especially little ones, even if she acts like she never saw any clothes other than the cotton things with sleeves that she wears like they were taken in to fit her. But if that's so, then somebody in that house is a good seamstress because the stitching's just as straight as a tailor's; but you know, Naomi never even uses makeup. Now that's something Mrs. Johnson hadn't really thought of before, but here's a teenage girl who's never even tried lipstick, and wouldn't you think that in this day and age . . .

"Yes, ma'am. Can you tell me anything about Mr. Wilson?"

Mr. Wilson is an appliance repairman somewhere, and he must make pretty good money to feed that bunch for as long as they've stayed. But except for Mrs. Wilson's sisters, they never have any visitors of any kind that she, Cheryl Johnson, can see. Not that she's nosy enough to care, but living right next door like this on a short street, you get to recognize everybody's car, and when a new one parks at the curb, you know it right away. Like yours—

when you pulled up, it was a strange car, and I said to myself, that's some kind of official car, the way it's painted so plain and ugly like that.

"Yes, ma'am. Is this Mr. Wilson?" He showed her the touched-up photograph of the corpse.

It seems a lot like him, but he's not as old as that picture makes him look. In fact that picture makes him look—oh my God, is he dead?

"Yes, ma'am. Did the Wilsons ever say anything about maybe moving somewhere? Maybe going somewhere else?"

"Dead? My God! I mean, it's not like he's a friend, but he always says good morning, and my God! How did it happen?"

"He was shot, ma'am. Anything at all about where they came from, or any names of friends they mentioned?"

"Shot? Oh my God!"

It took Wager another quarter-hour to find out that Mrs. Johnson didn't know what the world was coming to when a nice, polite man like Mr. Wilson, who never harmed anybody and minded his own business, could be shot down like that, and what was he—Detective Wager—doing to help make the streets safe? Did he know that she was getting afraid to even walk around the block at night because of all the terrible things that were happening? Shootings. Rapes. Assaults for no reason. Something had to be done, and now that nice Mr. Wilson. What about her children? What kind of world would they be faced with if things kept going the way they were?

"Yes, ma'am. Any kind of address or even just mentioning a town or city?"

No, the family next door never said a word about going anywhere. They were just gone, like that, as quick as they came. My God that poor Mrs. Wilson and her children.

Wager sat in his car, radio off and windows rolled up, to

enjoy a couple minutes of silence. Now his ears felt as worn
and grainy as his eyes, and beneath the weariness he felt
the start of one of those dull headaches that come from too
little sleep and no breakfast. And too much housewife's
mouth. Switching on the transmitter, and aware of the gap
in Mrs. Johnson's curtains, he called in for a search warrant
for the Beauchamp/Wilson address; a few minutes later
the dispatcher informed him that one had been signed
and duly recorded. Did he need a copy of it? Did he need
Technical Assistance?

"No," said Wager, "just authorization." He still had the
little tool of hooked and rippling blades that had come in
so handy when he was in the narcotics section, and that
would make the Bulldog very uneasy if he found out about
it. So Wager didn't tell him.

The front door had a deadbolt lock newly cut into the
wood above the original door handle, which had its own
lock. It took him two or three minutes' tinkering before
the last tumbler was finally lifted and held in place so he
could turn the mechanism. The door-handle latch took
half a second with the flat blade. The moment the door
swung in, a puff of odor and the sound of busy flies told him
that the Beauchamp/Wilson tribe was still at home.

Not even Detective Ross had a smartassed comment. No
one who entered the small house wanted to open his
mouth to breathe, let alone talk. Wager had been able to
make only a quick survey of the main floor before rushing
for the less-tainted air of the front porch and radioing
Homicide for the new duty watch. The only ones who
came prepared were Baird and his assistant; they wore
industrial masks over nose and mouth. Ross and Devereaux made do with alcohol-soaked handkerchiefs

wrapped about their faces like cowboys. Lincoln Jones held up until he reached the four kids and older girl tumbled over each other in the basement bathroom, where it looked as though they tried to hide. There he puked into the sink, trying not to splatter the small arms and legs tangled in the shower stall or the girl pressing a child between her and the toilet bowl gummy with smears of thick blood. Even Doyle came down to see this one.

"What do you mean they were the man's wives, Wager? All three of them?"

Tiredly, he went over it for the chief and wished to God that the Bulldog would throw away the half-smoked cigar he chewed on wetly. But Doyle didn't. Instead he twisted it half a turn and absently brushed away the cold ash that flecked his jacket. "An execution? You're calling this an execution?"

"That's right."

"A religious goddamn sacrifice?"

"An execution for religious purposes. Like Beauchamp. They even drew an avenging angel on the living-room wall."

"God."

That he wasn't too sure of. It took a lot more faith than he had to blame this on a god of any kind. It was simply human, and there the responsibility rested. There, too, the punishment would rest.

Beyond Doyle's car a second ambulance waited; the first was being loaded with sheeted figures trundled on gurneys down the short step of the front porch. Many of the lumps were small. The attendants worked quickly, pausing at the doorway for a deep breath before plunging back into the house. At a distance on both sides of the street, housewives and small children stood silent or sat on the curbs and watched; a mail truck puttered without moving as the bearded driver stared, and at the nearest intersection cars were already starting to nose toward the crowd of flashing lights. In her doorway hung Mrs. Johnson's face, mouth finally stilled in a slack-jawed O.

Wager fought another yawn and groaned as he rubbed his watering eyes. He thought the groan had been silent, but the Bulldog looked over at him.

"You were on duty last night?"

"Yessir."

"Ross and Devereaux can handle it here. Can you come in at five this afternoon? I want every man in the division to go over this thing. This is one of the worst . . . In over thirty years, Wager, I've never . . ." He plugged the words with the soggy cigar butt and made a faint squishing noise.

"I can be there."

"Fine—go get some sleep, if you can. Oh—and let me remind you, you've already built up more overtime than you can be compensated for. This will have to go under the 'service to community' category."

"I'm not worried about comp time." Or the goddamn activity forms.

"That's what I figured." When Doyle joined over thirty years ago, cops were on call twenty-four hours a day and never asked for compensatory time. That was before the union, the one Wager still hadn't joined. In some ways he and Doyle understood each other.

Wager heaved the car door open and was half out when he heard a familiar voice tell someone, "Get the house—wait until they're bringing out another one, and then get a full face of the house. What's all this about killer angels, Wager? What're you trying to hide from the public this time?"

"Screw you, Gargan."

"That's enough, Gabe," said Doyle. "You're off duty. I'll

see you at five." Then to Gargan, "I'll be liaison with the press on this one, Mr. Gargan. But let's wait until the television people get here so I only have to go over it once."

Wager slept. It was the total, motionless sleep of exhaustion, the kind you dive into as you drop onto the bed, and when your eyes shut you hear it coming fast, like an approaching train, and it roars over you. The next thing you hear is the alarm. You drag yourself across the bed to grope for the sound, your gummed lids sorely trying to squint open against the splintery feeling in your eyeballs. With one hand wrapped around the still-quivering clock, you take a few deep breaths and open your eyes a blink or two, a little longer each time, until they stay open enough for you to focus on the clock without tears blurring the red glow of numbers: 4:15. A steaming shower, a frozen dinner heated up to perfection, a hot and traffic-snarled scramble across town, and Wager stepped out of the elevator and into the eighth-floor conference room five minutes early. Max was already seated at the lower corner of the long table, where he could have room to sprawl his knees and elbows.

"Jumping Jesus, Gabe, you look awful."

"I don't feel awful. I feel pretty damn good." Which wasn't a lie, though it didn't help to have someone say he shouldn't.

Munn put some kind of tablet in his mouth and chewed it slowly. It left a little white scum at the corners of his mouth. "He don't look so bad."

Down the glossy table Ross sat busily jotting things on one of the yellow tablets that Doyle's secretary had sprinkled around the table. Ross's partner—the one Wager could stand, Devereaux—gazed out the window toward the distant mountains with sad and unseeing eyes. He was a Catholic, one of the few family men left in the division, and he had four kids about the age of some of the victims.

"Where's the coffee?" Wager asked.

Max shook his head. "Doyle's secretary hasn't brought it yet."

"She won't," said Munn. "Doyle thinks we drink too much coffee. The police doctor said that, collectively, we have higher blood pressure than any other group of public servants." He belched softly. "Something more to worry about."

Golding bustled in, nodding to everyone at the table, even those who didn't nod back. He was followed by the section's new man, Ziegler, recently transferred from Burglary and still a little uneasy at division meetings.

"Max—" Golding whispered loudly down the table. "Max—I got something new you've got to try. I don't know how I ever got along without it. It's the greatest thing in the world for getting rid of tension: a biofeedback machine."

"A what?"

"Biofeedback. You plug yourself into it, see, and then you concentrate on relaxing different parts of your body. You get a sonic readout on these earphones that tells you how relaxed you really are. Man, I had tensions I didn't even know I had. But with this machine, you can actually hear your tensions leave. It's amazing, Max; you really got to get yourself one."

"This machine relaxes you?" asked Munn.

"No. You do that yourself. The readout only tells you when you do it right. It's amazing how much tension we have and we never even know it. This machine tells you things about your own body that you'd never learn otherwise—it really works!"

"Well," said Munn, "with my luck, I'd probably electro-
cute me."

"Naw, there's not that much juice in it. Look, I've tried
TM and est and even went to some Personal Relations
Seminars, and none of those worked as good as this machine for letting you know just where you're at. And it's
purely organic."

"How can a machine be organic?" Wager asked.

"Because it projects your inner being. It's like watching
what your soul is doing on television or something. It's a
. . . a religious experience! You come out of that kind of
relaxation, you feel like you've been reborn."

Wager would have been happy to be reborn with a cup
of coffee, but just as he shoved back his chair to get one,
Doyle entered.

"All right, gentlemen. You've all seen the afternoon papers; you know the press reaction to this slaughter. It's the
biggest local story since the tornadoes, and the wire services have picked it up nationally."

Wager hadn't seen the papers, but he didn't waste time
saying so. If anything in them was important Doyle would
repeat it sooner or later.

"I'm trying to keep the lid on this thing until we have
some kind of case. So I don't want any of you people
talking to reporters. Be polite"; his blue eyes rested on
Wager. "But refer all questions to me. I don't want anything coming down like all that crap in Atlanta, with newsmen tripping the police and police agencies stumbling
over each other's jurisdiction."

"Not to mention each other's asses," muttered Ross.

"Everything you hear in this room," Doyle continued,
"keep it confidential. And send the reporters to me—it's
one of the reasons I get such a munificent salary."

Golding chuckled loudly.

"All right, Phil. Tell us what you've come up with so far."

Ross cleared his throat and leafed back through the folded sheets of the tablet until he came to item one. "We have eleven victims, three adult women, the rest apparently juveniles ranging in age from maybe a year to approximately fifteen—five girls and three boys. The oldest was a girl, the youngest a boy. All were shot at close range by a large-caliber handgun, apparently a single weapon. I suspect the killers used a silencer since none of the neighbors remembered hearing shots, and that was a lot of shooting. Since silencers are hard to get, that supports the single-gun theory. Baird guesses they were killed maybe ten days ago, but the coroner hasn't had a chance to analyze the stomach contents, so we don't yet know what time of day. We figure there was more than one killer, since the shootings took place all at approximately the same time, and apparently nobody tried to escape. To judge by the location of the bodies, they were divided up into two groups. Let me draw this floor plan for you."

He went to the portable blackboard and, referring to his notes, sketched the rooms of the small house and its basement, placing X's for each of the bodies. "Now this isn't exact, but it's close enough, okay?"

"Can you give us your reconstruction?" Doyle asked.

"Yessir. We figure it's likely one killer was at the back door when the other or others knocked at the front. There was no sign of forced entry, except for Wager's little lock-picking trick. If the killer effected entry that way, any evidence of it has been violated."

"You think I should have kicked down the door, Ross?"

"We'll get to Gabe's part later. Go on, Phil."

"Yessir. Anyway, it looks like the victims let the killer or killers in through the front door. Whereupon the best guess is the killer pulled a gun and let in his accomplice or accomplices. No one made a run for it," he explained again to the men, who sat silently at the table looking at the chalk sketch. "If they hadn't had the exits covered somebody out of all those people would have made a run for the back door or a window."

"I agree. Go on."

"We think they then took the three adult women and sat them in the living room under guard, while an accomplice took the older children to the downstairs bathroom, which has no windows or other exit. Who got shot first, I don't know. But after the women were killed, and maybe the ones in the bathroom, the killers went through the bedrooms shooting the three littlest kids, who were sleeping there." He turned from pointing at those X's. "That place was like a dormitory—double, triple bunks everywhere. I don't know how in hell that many people lived in a house that size without going nuts. Anyway, we spent the whole goddamn day in that place marking and measuring, and we still don't have too much. Baird and his people are doing what they can with ballistics and fingerprints; the first coroner's reports should be coming in sometime tonight." Ross lifted the lapel of his coat and sniffed, making a sick face. "The goddamn smell—"

"Did you find any notes?" Wager asked. "A drawing of an angel with a sword?"

Ross looked down the table. "Your killer angel? Only the one you saw, Wager. Here, we took a picture of it." He passed along a Polaroid color photograph of the living-room wall. Daubed in brown streaks of dried blood and taller than a standing man, the familiar spread-winged angel towered over the flung body of a woman. Gazing at the picture, Wager saw what he hadn't had time to notice in his hasty tour through the room before calling in the homicides: this angel had a face. It was dominated by two round circles for eyes, and in the center of each startled ring was a single dot of blood—the pupils of an enraged, maddened stare.

"As you know from the papers, they're calling it the 'angel of death' murders, and they're doing their best to scare people shitless about it."

Munn crunched another tablet. "It scares hell out of me, Chief. Anybody killing women and children and decorating the walls with their blood, they got to be maniacs."

"I won't argue that. But Wager has some information that'll tell us what kind of maniacs. It's what sent him to that address in the first place, and it was a good piece of detective work. But next time, call Technical Assistance; don't use a lock pick. Go ahead—fill them in."

Wager was tired of telling the same story over and over and getting the same startled exclamations, "polygamy?" and "avenging angels?" But it was necessary and he did his best to hold his temper even when Golding went off on some half-assed dissertation about religious mania and a modern search for values. It didn't have one damn thing to do with finding out who butchered eleven women and children.

"So other than this drawing, you found nothing to link the Mueller killing to the others?" Doyle asked to get the talk back to the subject.

"No, sir. I also called Orvis down in Pueblo and brought him up to date, but he still doesn't have an address for his victim. I'd like to look through any letters or documents that Ross and Devereaux find—these people kept in touch with each other, and I suspect the killers knew that, too."

"Good God," muttered Axton. "Not another houseful."

Doyle made a note on a yellow pad.

Devereaux, who had been murmuring with Ross, caught Wager's eye. "We didn't have time to go through everything in the house, Gabe—we went after the more fragile evidence first. But the drawers we did look in were messed up. I think you're right—I think the killers were looking for some kind of lead to the Pueblo victim, and they obviously found it."

Ross added, "Baird's fingerprinting the whole house; with that many people, there's prints everywhere. He told me it'll take him all day tomorrow just to get prints from the victims. The kids', especially, had decayed pretty bad, and he says it'll take time to build them up. Anyway, he's still out there dusting the drawers and contents. Probably be half the night before he'll let us go through them."

Wager thought a moment. "What about telephone records? With a deuces tecum, we can subpoena a list of long-distance numbers billed to that phone."

"We could," said Ross. "And in fact I already thought of that. But one problem, Wager: no phone."

"All right," said Doyle. "This is obviously—"

The pop of every transmitter in the room interrupted him as the dispatcher called for the homicide officer on duty. "X-86, you have a 10-32 and a possible victim at Colfax and Emerson. Officers at the scene."

Munn groaned and answered that he was on his way.

Golding, on the same shift, quickly gathered his notes. "They're singing my song—sorry, Chief." And he was out the door behind Munn.

"Obviously," the Bulldog continued, "this is a case whose brutality makes it especially important. The mayor's asked for and received the governor's approval for a statewide task force to pursue the perpetrators. I will head that task force, DPD Homicide will provide the manpower. The attorney general's office will effect liaison with any and all local agencies we may be led into contact with. We have been assured that every district attorney will cooperate fully in this investigation. The governor has also asked the FBI to provide assistance in case interstate flight is involved, and he has been assured by neighboring states of the fullest cooperation of their agencies if we need it. We will go after these people as priority one. However, we will not let up on our other duties. It means extra work; it means more overtime if you're willing to give it. With the—ah—union rules, of course, I can't demand that. But I will find ways of—ah—compensating those who donate. Those who do not will not in any way be penalized, of course."

That was for Ross, the union rep for this division. Doyle went on to detail the assignments for the remaining detectives, most of which they had thought of anyway. Except maybe for Ziegler, whose Bic pen scratched busily: question every household along both sides of the street; nontechnical assistance for Baird's understaffed lab people; a central desk for information gathering and communications; visits to every grocery store or clothing store or medical center or pharmacy where the victims might have traded. Anything else that might fill in the routines of the victims' last day—and with it, anybody who might have seemed interested in them.

7.

It wasn't until the next morning, during one of those long, desultory stretches that usually come between two and four, that Wager had a chance to pay attention to the itch that had pestered him even while he sat in the car with Chief Doyle. The two of them had watched the sheeted figures carried out past the crowd of neighbors, the cars slowing to a halt at the distant intersection, the faces mute with shock . . . something about those faces . . . That crowded scene had been unlike the vacant streets Wager and Axton were cruising now, where the patrol car's headlights moved through the dark like prodding fingers touching nothing . . . Silent and preoccupied, Wager drove, the unmarked car creaking loudly as it bounced across the dips of intersections; Axton, equally silent, gazed at the lights sliding past. Finally he proved to Wager that, as so often in the past, they had been mulling over the same thing: "I still can't believe it—women, children, slaughtered like that. And for what reason?"

"The killers are God's angels," said Wager. "They go around doing favors for God."

Axton's thin whistle rode over the sporadic queries and replies on the radio.

"Don't you think, Gabe, that if the killers had found an address leading them to Pueblo we'd have heard about it by now?"

"If I hadn't known where to look, the Beauchamp family might still be rotting there."

"Yeah. You're right. Crap." Then Max added, "The Kruse family probably know how to hide as well as the Beauchamps. For all the good it did them."

Which is what sharpened the little itch: the Beauchamps had been good at hiding. Clever people. In the first place, they were adept at masking their way of life from even their closest neighbors; and they were practiced at evading the hunters they knew were on their trail. Yet they had kept in touch with the others—they wrote to Zenas Winston, perhaps called the Kruses in Pueblo from pay phones. They must have kept in touch with the Kruses down there because the killers had found something to lead them as far as Kruse himself. Letters—the mailman with his little blue and white cart putting from house to house and stopping to stare with the rest of the neighborhood at the ambulances and the line of sheeted figures. The Beauchamps must have written letters and received letters, but they stayed hidden . .

"You in a hurry to get home after work?"

"Why?" asked Max.

"Post box," said Wager. "If I was Beauchamp and wanted to be sure nobody knew where to find my family I'd use a post office box for an address."

Axton heaved a deep breath of agreement. "Yeah. And under a different name!" Then, "Central Post Office?"

"We can start there."

They did, after turning the watch over to Ross and Devereaux, who were on their way out to the Beauchamp neighborhood to begin canvassing for any witnesses they had not yet interviewed.

"You don't want to tell Ross where we're going?" Max asked innocently.

"The case started with us," said Wager.

"Right," said Max. "And them with brains gets the gains."

The Central Post Office was not far, but the drive through heavy morning traffic, tangled by the streets blocked for construction of the new downtown mall, took over half an hour. By the time they arrived at the Greek-style building with its stone lions and columns, lines of people had formed in front of slow-moving clerks, and Axton groaned, "Christ, it'll take all day."

"The hell it will. We've already put in a day's work." He led Max past the mail windows and the long wall of post boxes toward a small corridor bearing the sign SUPERINTENDENT. In an anteroom a secretary looked up without smiling.

"Yes?"

Wager flashed his badge. "We'd like permission to show this photograph to your clerks. It's a homicide victim."

"Well I certainly can't give that kind of permission!"

"Yes, ma'am." Axton smiled. "But what about the superintendent?"

"He's not in yet."

They waited, Wager feeling both the night's weariness and his anger rise as the slow minutes passed. At a quarter past nine the superintendent came in, a florid man who assumed that any new face in his office meant one more problem he could do without. "My clerks? You want every one of my clerks to see if they recognize this guy?"

"It's related to that mass murder in the papers yesterday —the women and children," said Wager.

"I don't care if it's related to World War III, those people out there are busy. And," he pointed out, "this here's a federal building, and you're not the FBI."

"The FBI has offered to help if we need it." Wager himself heard the Spanish lilt in his voice. "But I wouldn't want to call them down here just because you did not cooperate on a routine request. They'll have reports to file, letters of explanation. The kind of thing that goes in personnel records."

"I don't give a damn—"

"All we need to know," interrupted Axton gently, "is if anyone remembers renting a box to this man."

"That's all you want? Hell, you don't need to pester all my clerks for that—we got only two windows that rent boxes. Next time say what you want." After a brief, angry silence he flapped a hand at his secretary. "Take them down there, Ann." The door to the inner office slammed shut behind him. She eyed Wager and Axton as if they had spoiled the office picnic. "Follow me."

Four clerks took turns working the windows that serviced the boxes. None recalled Beauchamp.

"We don't usually see the customers after they rent their box," said a bony man with graying hair and eyes set into deep sockets. "Unless they get a lot of packages or registered mail—the stuff that brings them to the window."

Axton nodded. "Do you know what post office would serve this address?" He showed the clerk the Beauchamp house number.

"Just a minute; I'll check." He took the address and disappeared somewhere behind a partition.

"That's the guy who should be superintendent," murmured Axton.

"He's too nice," said Wager. "The secretary has my vote." It was the kind of verbal silliness that came when you were bone-tired but the adrenaline was pumping because there was a chance—however faint—that something was going to pay off.

When the bony man came back he said, "The South Denver substation—255 South Broadway."

They nosed through the crowded parking area, finally locating a slot. "It's another federal jurisdiction," said Max. "You want to call the FBI?"

"Naw, let's just use our good looks and friendly dispositions."

"Right—look how far they've got us already."

This station had a single long window served by three or four clerks who called "next" to the line of waiting customers. There was no door marked Supervisor or Office, so Axton and Wager stood behind a short, heavy lady who smelled of old sweat. When their turn came, Wager showed his badge and the photograph.

The clerk, wearing a checked civilian shirt open at the neck, slowly shook his head. "I don't think so . . . maybe . . . but I can't be sure."

"Would you show it to the rest of the people? It's very important."

He shrugged but did, moving down the row of clerks as a disgusted whisper came from somewhere in the line behind Wager, "What the hell now!"

When the clerk came back, he bobbed his head toward the last station. "Henry says he recognizes him."

"Thanks." Wager was already halfway down the counter.

Henry had a round face, bald on top, with a full, pointed beard that made him look like a shovel. Wager stood by restlessly as the smelly woman counted pennies for her short string of stamps, then he showed his badge. "What can you tell me about this man?"

The clerk shrugged. "He got a box, let's see . . . nine or ten months ago. He wanted to pay by the month instead of quarterly—that's how I remember him. He made a thing of it, but we only accept quarterly payments. It cuts the billing costs, and most people if they're only going to be here a month use general delivery."

"Can you tell me anything about him? When he came in? If you ever saw anybody with him?"

Henry thought back. "When he did come in, it was usually midafternoon, I guess. Slack-time—not many customers. That's when I'd notice him, anyway. And always by himself."

"Do you remember his name?"

"Dawson? Doggett?"

"Do you know which box he rented?"

"I guess I could go through the cards and see if his name comes up. But that's gonna take some time." He glanced at the line of people waiting silently.

"It has to do with that mass murder of women and children."

"Oh! God, I read about that." He looked at the photo, then back at Wager. "This guy might be the killer?"

"Another victim," said Wager.

"Oh—okay, hang on a minute."

It took more than a minute. Almost ten, in fact, before Henry came back with a file card. "Drayman. Edward B. Drayman. I knew it started with a D, but I had the rest of it wrong. I'm better on faces than I am on names. Maybe I shouldn't be a mailman."

"That's okay—that's fine—what's the box number?"

"Fifteen twenty-two. But I can't let you in it. It's the U.S. Mails. You need a warrant or something."

"We'll get one. Thanks again."

Axton scanned the wall full of little glass and steel doors for 1522; when he found it, he turned to Wager and grinned. "Bingo!"

Wager, too, looked. Against the other side of the glass panel leaned a small stack of envelopes. "Now let's see what Doyle can do for us," said Wager. "Unless you're ready to knock off for the day."

"I'm ready to see what's in that mailbox, my man." He moved with surprising quickness out to the Trans-Am baking in the morning sun; Wager used his GE radio pack to call in, and the Bulldog's voice returned, blurry through some kind of electronic interference halfway across Denver.

"You want to spell the name the box is under?"

Wager did.

"All right—I'll bring the warrant myself."

He did, within the hour, and found Wager and Axton half asleep in the hot car.

"No problem with the Feds this time," said Doyle, his lower teeth thrusting out happily. "Full cooperation."

It wasn't always like that Wager knew; in narcotics and organized crime, the Feds held their cards pretty close to the chest and didn't want the locals to see much of them. But he guessed that Doyle used the notoriety of this case to get good cooperation—who wouldn't want to help capture a slayer of women and children?

The station superintendent had never before seen a federal warrant and had to call for instructions from the Central Post Office. They were slow in coming, even over the telephone, and the voice at the other end—as stout and sullen as it had been earlier this morning—asked three times for the name of the federal judge who signed the paper. Finally he said, "I guess so," and the local superintendent, still frowning worriedly at the warrant, said to Doyle, "Come with me, sir."

He was back in a minute. The three men huddled over an empty writing shelf to gaze at the envelopes. They were all addressed to Edward B. Drayman. One, Wager recognized: Winston, Rt. 6, Box 81, Loma Vista, Colo. Another lacked a return address. The last two were from A. Cooney, Box 2013, Pueblo, Colo.

"That must be it," said Axton. "A box number and an alias—Kruse used the same technique as Beauchamp."

"Worked about as well, too," said Wager.

"Can we open them?" asked Max.

"The warrant didn't specify," Doyle answered.

Wager unfolded his pocket knife. "Then it doesn't say not to."

Carefully holding the envelope by a corner, he slit the top seam. The letters were penned in blue ball-point on lined paper; they talked about the health and troubles of a dozen names, and offered the answers to questions Beauchamp had asked in earlier letters. At the bottom of the second letter Kruse had written, "Thank you for sending Z's warning about W though it is scarcely needed. The Lord will guide and protect. Our faith like yours is in the goodness of the Lord. His will be done."

"Does that mean anything?" Doyle pointed at the W.

"Willis Beauchamp," said Wager. " 'Z' is probably Zenas Winston, and he wrote to warn that Willis was after them."

The Bulldog squeaked a bit of air between two teeth. "It's not much, but it may lead to motive."

The chief was already thinking trial, which was fine; but Wager figured they'd have to catch somebody first. "I'll go

down to Pueblo," he told Doyle. "I can call this information to Orvis, and by the time he gets a street address for
the Kruse family, I can be there."

"I can go," said Max. "You went last time."

"It'll be more consistent if I go," said Wager. "Orvis and
I know each other. Besides, Polly's barbecue's coming up;
if you're not around to help her plan that we'll have the
murder of Max-the-Ax on our hands."

"Very funny."

"Gabe's right," Doyle said. "Let's see what we've got in
these other letters, then you get on down there."

He met Detective Orvis at the Pueblo police station, a
two-story building of tan brick whose design was institu-
tional ugly, which made Wager feel at home. Parking was
down a graveled alley and into the scorched and unfenced
lot behind the building. As he walked to the entry under
the large PUEBLO POLICE DEPARTMENT sign, Wager noted
an attempt to soften the brick face with a few sickly trees
and one window that had frilled curtains and a potted
geranium on the sill. It must have been the policewomen's
lounge. Orvis's office was in the annex, next building
north; the architect for this one did his best to match the
main building, and succeeded. A uniformed officer
pointed him down the waxed hall to Orvis's office, where
Wager found a man who was slightly taller and maybe ten
years younger than himself. He had a quick handshake
and a wide mustache that matched his brown hair. And he
wanted Wager to know that despite Denver's interest in
the Kruse shooting and the establishment of a statewide
task force, this case was still in his territory. "We haven't
yet come up with a street address on that post office box,"
he said. "Kruse put a fictitious street number on the appli-

cation, so we're canvassing the area around the substation for people who might recognize him. It might take some time," he apologized. "We're short-handed. We don't get all the federal funds you people in Denver get."

They didn't have all the criminal activity that Denver had, either, but Wager let it slide. He was after cooperation, not a quarrel. The politeness lasted through two cups of coffee and a tour of the facility, including a new central communications room that they were very proud of. But Orvis, like Wager, was restless, and when Wager suggested that he could help with the door-to-door, the Pueblo detective grinned with relief and drove them out to the neighborhood.

By late afternoon Orvis and Wager were working down both sides of a street lined with houses built of dark brown brick. They all had identical tiny porches in front and detached garages down the dirt alley behind: a row of workers' cottages, probably built for the steel-mill crews at the beginning of the century. They were still filled with kids and housewives, now mostly Hispanic instead of Italian; and as Wager knocked and showed Kruse's picture and asked the same fruitless question, he heard the sounds of his own childhood, and smelled the odors of familiar cooking as the homes began to prepare for their men's return.

Perhaps it was the result of another long day after little sleep, perhaps it was the disjointed locations of the past few days, but Wager once again felt a jolting shift of time, this one into his own memory. In the wide, dark eyes of children peeping from behind their mothers' knees, he saw faces familiar from his boyhood before the Auraria barrio had been swept away by machines. In the frayed chalk lines on broken slabs of sidewalk, he saw the games that had filled the long summer twilights when kids liked to gather in groups, hoping their parents would forget to call them in to bed. Even the trees, cottonwoods with thick twisted trunks whose bark was polished with the rub of familiar hands, brought memories of cool shade on sun-scorched afternoons, and quiet play—making pictures in the gray sand or building rock houses and forts for ants and beetles to live in. Of the soft, unformed faces that, like his own, had somehow grown up and scattered away. Those memories were such a long way from knocking on screen doors with their little wad of cotton to scare away the flies, such a distance—from such a different direction, even—that he could not clearly trace what led from an alien and wide-eyed kid to homicide detective Wager, a man for whom the past was now found only through the lives of others, and through nothing in himself. The isolated man. His ex-wife had thought of him as that. So, in her own way, did Jo. And Max. Wager even admitted it about himself. He was an isolated man trying to keep his goals limited to what he could set his hands on. There was nothing wrong in that—it was just a fact, one that Wager was truly com-fortable with. And now, ironically, he was pursuing a peo-ple who scorned all goals except the abstract one of completing God's design—a people for whom his kind of isolation was as foreign as their kind of union was to him.

He reached the end of the block and was about to cross into the next, a collection of frame houses built at different times, when the nasal quack of Orvis's radio caught his ear. Looking, he saw Orvis beckon, and even halfway across the street the man's smile was widely visible.

"We got a positive, Detective Wager. Over near Craig and Thirteenth. It's just a few blocks."

They found the uniformed officer chatting with a lady who half filled a wooden porch swing. Her iron-colored hair was clipped short all around, and the bulk of her breasts and stomach and hips made the cotton dress taut across her flesh. The officer, sitting on the edge of the porch with a cold glass of tea, wiped his hatband with a handkerchief as he told Orvis about it.

"This is Mrs. Tillotson. She says Kruse lives behind her on the next street over."

"You're sure it's the same man?"

"Well, I didn't know his name. But I saw him enough. Almost every day for six months. Him and his wife and children and her sister, too. You boys want some ice tea? It's awfully hot today."

"Can you show us the house?" Orvis asked.

She grunted herself out of the swing, whose chains twanged slack. "Only take a minute to get you your ice tea. That house ain't going anywhere no matter where the people went."

"How's that?"

"They left. Couple weeks ago now. Children, dog, everyone—just up and left like they meant to come back, but they ain't. Not yet."

"Did you see them go?" asked Wager.

"No. But if you don't see me go you won't get that ice tea."

Wager and Orvis glanced at each other.

The woman, tugging her dress down in back, went into the shadowy house.

"Go on around back," Wager said to the patrolman. "See if you smell anything."

"Smell?"

Wager nodded. "They might still be there."

"Oh?" Then, "Oh, Lord!" The patrolman swallowed uneasily and peeked down the driveway beside the house. "Maybe there's a dog back there."

"Here you boys are, nice and cold. Why, you ain't going yet, are you, Officer?"

"Yes, ma'am—I thought I'd cut through the yard and see which house you meant."

"Oh, land sakes, sit down. I'll show you just as soon's you finish that ice tea. There's too much rushing around, and it's just too hot for it."

"Ma'am—"

"Sit, young man!"

"Did you ever talk to the family, ma'am?" Orvis asked.

"Sure. All the time. They hang out their wash, I hang out mine. They have plenty of it, too. Nice folks, though. Just as friendly."

"They ever say where they came from?"

"No. Can't say that. We just talk. Recipes, kids' sicknesses, whatall. My! You boys were so thirsty and all I been doing is talking. Here, let me get you some more."

"No thanks, ma'am. It was real good. But if you'll just show us the house."

"Well, if you got to . . ."

"Yes, ma'am."

"Well, it's right behind my place. Here, we can go right through the yard. There's gates." She walked with the caution of a heavy person afraid to stumble and fall. The uniformed officer reached for one of her elbows when they came to the rougher ground of the backyard. "Oh, my, ain't you kind though!"

They followed across the stubbled clump grass and between two laden apple trees to an unpainted gate hanging slack in a rusty wire fence. The uniformed officer occasionally sniffed loudly.

"Right there—just across the alley." She pointed to a backyard bound by a picket fence that still showed flakes of white paint. Wager saw the scattering of children's toys, the holes and sand piles of kids' aimless digging, the silence of the house's long shadow.

"Let's find out," he said.

The uniformed officer volunteered, "Let me take you back, ma'am."

"Oh, my!"

No one answered their knock at either door. Drawing a deep breath, Wager put his nose to the keyhole and sniffed lightly.

"Well?" asked Orvis.

"I don't smell anything."

Orvis went to one of the windows and cupped his hands around his reflection to peer in. "I don't see anybody. Let's get legal."

By the time the warrant arrived, Wager and Orvis had interviewed the people living on both sides of the house. Yes, they recognized Kruse, but his name was Hartley. They were a friendly bunch of people who nonetheless kept to themselves and never said anything about where they came from. They never bothered anybody, but if somebody needed something they'd help out. Good, quiet neighbors. One morning they packed up and went, and everybody expected them back. But that was a couple weeks ago now.

"Did they have a car?"

"A pickup with a camper shell that they barely fit into. Mrs. Hartley, her younger sister, and their five kids and a dog. A blue GMC, it was. The dog's name was Elmer."

"Mr. Hartley wasn't with them?"

"No—is he the one that got shot? Is this the picture that was in the paper a while back?"

"Yes, ma'am."

"You know, I thought at the time that could be him, but I never really believed it was! It looks a lot more like him here than it did in the paper, and he was such a nice man, always said hello. I never dreamed anybody like that could get shot."

The house was empty. The drawers hung open and were stripped; the refrigerator contained only moldering scraps of food; the washing machine on the back porch held a wad of clothes forgotten and now dried into a hard tangle.

"They got away. It looks like they made it," said Orvis.

Wager, too, felt a surge of relief. "Now we want to find them before the avenging angels do."

There were the usual ways of looking for missing persons, and Detective Orvis took care of those: an all-points for the vehicle if it was still in the state; an interagency query in case it moved across the line; a national missing-persons alert for possible victims matching the following descriptions. . . . Wager, after calling Chief Doyle and reporting his findings, placed a call to Loma Vista and Sheriff Tice.

"I seen that bulletin on the murder of the Beauchamps, Detective Wager. I'm glad to hear the Kruse people got away."

"Do you have any idea where they might go?"

"No, I don't. I'll ask around, though. And I'll tell the deputies to keep an eye out for their truck in case they come this way. But if it's been two weeks now they probably found a place to hole up. And that could be anywhere."

"I think the killers are still after them."

"Yes, so do I. And we'll do what we can, Detective Wager. Our district attorney got word from the attorney general that we're supposed to help you people all we can."

"We appreciate that, Sheriff. You know about the state-wide task force set up for this thing?"

"Not much. Suppose you tell me about that."

Wager did, mentioning casually that Bulldog Doyle was coordinating it.

"Doyle? I don't know that I ever met him. But you tell him I'll be glad to work with you—you seem to know what you're doing and how we do things over here. You even got Orrin to take you over to the benchland, didn't you?"

Wager was no longer surprised at the osmosis of news in Loma Vista. "Yes. But it didn't do much good with the Mueller killing. The people I talked to didn't know why Mueller would be linked to the avenging angels or to Beauchamp."

"That's what I been telling you."

"You don't have anything more, then?"

"Absolutely nothing. Have you talked to Orrin since you found the Beauchamps?"

"No."

"You ought to. Wait a minute—I'll get you his phone number."

When Wager finally reached Orrin at the newspaper office, the newsman said he'd read about the Beauchamp family in the morning papers. "In fact, I took a copy over for Zenas to read. It makes the both of us sick, Gabe."

"I'd have called sooner, but I haven't had time. I'm in Pueblo now. We finally located Kruse's house. It looks like his family got away in time."

"Thank the Lord!"

And a fast GMC pickup. "We're trying to reach them before the avenging angels do. Have you any idea where they might run?"

"No, I don't."

"They must have had a place picked out," Wager insisted. "Everything else is so well planned that they must have planned for this possibility, too."

"That makes sense, Gabe. But, Lord, I don't know. Something like that, they wouldn't tell anybody, probably not even Zenas."

That was so. "Can you talk to Zenas? See if he can come up with some guesses? Anything at all—if we find them we can protect them. If we don't it's only a matter of time."

"Gabe, these people don't want your protection—they've been running from the law all their lives."

"But they're not polygamists anymore; they're widows and orphans. I don't know any goddamn law against being widows of the same man."

"Well . . ."

"And Zenas sent you to me, didn't he? He wasn't shy about asking help when he was scared, was he?"

"No, he wasn't. That's true. Okay, I'll go over. . . . Let's see, tomorrow's distribution day. . . . I can go over as soon as I get loose tomorrow afternoon. Where can I call you if I find out something?"

"Go through Tice's office. He's got a number for the task force—they'll reach me."

There was one more call Wager had to make, but it was a personal one and it kept until he was flat on his back on the hard bed of a motel room. His belly was full of something called "beef-tips Burgundy," and the muscles of his neck and back were finally relaxing from the pummeling of a hot shower.

"Jo—it's me, Gabe."

"Hi, stranger! I heard about you finding that family who was shot. That must have been terrible."

"Just another day at the office. Listen, I wanted to call and apologize for not coming by last night—I tried to call, but you weren't home."

"I was over at Mother's. I left you a note."

"I found it. It was the only thing in there besides ads and bills." That didn't sound quite right. "It was good to find it," he added lamely.

"Why, Gabe! That's downright romantic!"

"Let's not get too damn sentimental."

"All right." A touch of apology under the laughter in her voice. "Come on over; I'll feed you and rub your back before you go on duty."

"I can't. I'm down in Pueblo. Doyle told me to stay here tonight. He's afraid I'll fall asleep at the wheel." Suddenly everybody was worrying about his health. Maybe he was beginning to look old and frail. Wager had never thought about becoming old and frail, like one of the skinny, bent men with white hair and dark wrinkled faces that used to shuffle around the barrio when he was a kid. They'd gather on the warm side of a wall, sitting on tilted chairs in the morning sun and swapping the same jokes and tales they'd shared since they were wet-nosed kids running around in the same streets. Now, of course, those streets were no more, nor was there a place to sit and re-create a past. Any old men remaining were hidden away from the little boys who used to squat nearby to listen. Now there was progress.

"I said when are you coming back?"

"Tomorrow morning. I'll drop by."

"Okay." She added, tentatively, "It'll be good to see you."

"And you."

8.

It was good to see Jo. Wager arrived in Denver just in
time to take her to lunch at My Brother's Bar, just up
I-25 from Mile-Hi Stadium—Bears' Stadium it was called
before professional football caught on. The tavern was
run by a quietly smiling Greek, and the music was classi-
cal stuff, which Wager liked because it was quiet and interesting even if he didn't know what it was, and even if,
with this crowd, you couldn't hear it very well. The tavern spread through two large rooms filled with heavy tables and did not have a single fern. Despite the noon
swarm of blow-dried salesmen and young lawyers wan-
dering in from historically salvaged lower downtown, the
place still gave Wager the sense of community he had
enjoyed at the old Frontier Bar before it was torn down.
He tried to explain that feeling to Jo and to apologize for
the noise and people—it was a different place in midafternoon or later in the evening. But he saw that the only
thing she was really interested in was the sound of his
voice and not what it said. Which, he decided, wasn't too
bad; so the lunch, if hurried and noisy and jostled, was a

fine one, though he could not tell you what they ate.

When he dropped her off at the police complex, he surprised them both by kissing her hard under the amused glances of office cops returning from lunch.

"I suppose that's the result of getting a good night's sleep."

He shook his head. "Just the result of being with you. Maybe," he added, ". . . maybe it's a feeling of refuge. Everywhere—so much, so fast . . ."

"I never thought of you as feeling that way," she said.

"What way?"

"Feeling that you could be whirled away. I always think of you as a rock."

She had stated exactly the way he felt, and there came again that sense of completeness with her, of sharing even those thoughts that had not yet been clearly formulated. But despite that warmth, he found it hard to admit her to an area that was intensely private as well as subject to his own ridicule. "Right, a rock: silent, hardheaded, and always on somebody's toes."

"You're starting to sound as cynical as Gargan."

"That bastard."

"Do you really feel that way sometimes? Uprooted?"

"I guess. Sometimes. It used to be it was enough to be a good cop. You knew who and what you were and how good you were at it." He added, "I lost a wife in order to be a good cop, and it wasn't her fault."

"Or yours."

"That's nice to say. But not true. I told her either she changed or she got the hell out."

Jo gazed out the car window at the massive concrete slabs that formed the blank, gray face of the police building's lower floor. "Just like that?"

"Pretty close. She wasn't important at the time."

"Oh."

"Now maybe she would be. And I'd be less of a cop."

"I can't imagine you being less of a cop. Or anything being more important to you than that." Her dark eyes turned to his. "But I can imagine you being lonely. It's tough to have to be right all the time—to think that you have to be too hard to make a mistake."

"I'm not feeling sorry for myself, Jo."

"And I'm not trying to mother you. It's just hard to be alone. Like it's hard to learn you're not important to someone you . . . believed you were important to. I just never thought of you worrying about those things—you seem so self-contained, so complete in what you do and who you are."

"I am." He tapped the steering wheel for emphasis. "I am!"

"But now you want something more, is that it?"

"I don't know. I really don't." He tried to put it into words as much for himself as for her. "I think of that whole family wiped out—the Beauchamps—kids who never even had a chance to enjoy the world . . . to even see the goddamn world . . . ." His hand tightened to a fist on the wheel. "Jo, if I could pull the switch on their killers I'd feel completely, totally happy. I want them that bad, and right now that's all I want!" The fist slackened. "And yet, in a way, those dead kids had more than I've got—call it a history, a bunch of people they shared their lives with. I look around and suddenly things have changed so much . . . I don't have that kind of history anymore—this isn't the town I grew up in. The old neighborhood's gone—places I used to be at home in. Even the mountains are changing. I guess I feel like I could disappear, like everything else, and it wouldn't make a ripple anywhere. Except," he reached for her cold hand, "except when I'm with you. Then it feels like I—we—could build something that wouldn't change. Something that wouldn't give in to . . . chaos."

They both looked at her hand lying in his. Finally she asked, "Is that a kind of proposal?"

"No!"

"I didn't think it was." Her laugh was forced.

And he did not know how to make that reflexive answer sound less bad.

"Let's call it 'midcase depression,'" she said, opening the door quickly.

"I'll phone tonight."

"If you want to."

Even in the glare of afternoon sunlight against the balcony curtains, the red light on his telephone recorder was sharp. Pressing Rewind and Play, he listened to Doyle's secretary's voice tell him that he had a message via the Loma Vista sheriff's office: one Orrin Winston wants Wager to call as soon as possible, followed by a telephone number. Time, 10:39. He tried. A woman's twangy voice at the distant end told him that Orrin had left the office to go over to the benchland somewhere, but had not said when he would be back. Would he like to leave a message?

"Just tell him Gabe Wager called from Denver. I'll try to get him at home later."

"Okay. I know he wanted to talk to you. I'll leave a note."

He called Doyle's office next. Doyle's secretary brought him up to date on the new facts, and there wasn't much: "Detective Devereaux got a description of the Beauchamps' car, a Country Squire station wagon, blue or gray and sort of beat up. No license number."

"Motor Vehicles have anything turn up?"

"No abandoned cars matching that description."

The secretary's voice was beginning to echo the cadence of her boss's. Wager had noticed elsewhere that people who shared the same office and heard each other on the telephone month after month began to speak alike. But as long as she didn't try to share Doyle's authority toward his people, or smoke cheap cigars, he could stomach her. "What about NCIC? Anything come in yet on fingerprints?"

"All the prints so far belong to the victims. Detective Ross believes the killers wore gloves. Probably surgical-type."

Surgical gloves, silencers, persistence, planning. The avenging angels were turning out to be very good in their line of business. So good that it was going to take something special to catch them. Special effort, special skill, and even special luck.

That was the thought he carried with him as he puttered around his apartment, giving it the monthly swipe with a vacuum cleaner, sniffing the towels and sheets to see if they needed washing this week, rattling Saran-wrapped plates and bowls in the refrigerator to toss out the blue-green fuzzy wads that he had forgotten about. He dumped a bowl of something slimy that had once been liquid. Buffalo soup. There was an old recipe for buffalo soup that began, First you catch a buffalo. So far they hadn't even set a trap.

At six he called Jo. "You want some dinner?"

"Not tonight, Gabe. I think I'll wash my hair and read a book."

"Jo—look, I'm sorry about this afternoon." Why in hell did a man always end up telling some woman he was sorry for something? Mothers, sisters, girlfriends, wives, mistresses—the whole damn progression.

"That's all right, Gabe. I shouldn't have kidded about that."

And they always said it was all right when it wasn't.

How in God's name did a polygamist manage? "It's a whole mixture of things, Jo. I've never been able to talk to anyone about a lot of things that are important to me. It started a long time ago, when I was a kid. It's just something I can't help." The line remained silent. "It's not just marriage, Jo—it's," he groped for a word that would sound neither pretentious nor trite, but only came up with "life."

"I know that, Gabe."

Well, if she knew everything, there wasn't much sense trying to explain anything. Wager said something about seeing her tomorrow morning and she said something about his having a good tour of duty and they hung up. Leaving him to stare at the silent telephone as if it were a mechanism that consciously twisted words out of their meaning and intent. Someday he would have to figure how much time he spent talking to machines instead of to people. And trying to talk to people but sounding like a machine. That part would be easy—there weren't many he talked to that he considered people. Sighing, he dialed another number, a long-distance exchange, and listened to the switches click automatically into the rattle of a bell. A woman's voice said, "Hello?"

"Mrs. Winston?"

"Yes?"

"This is Gabe Wager in Denver. Is Orrin home yet?"

"No, he's not, Mr. Wager. I know he wanted to talk to you, though. He should be back soon. Does he have your number?"

Wager gave her his unlisted home number and then lay on the bed in the half light of pulled drapes and tried to force some stillness into a mind that persisted in churning: phrases, images, fragments of the past mixing with twisted and half-formed glimpses of the future. The case, his own life, the victims, Jo—all tangled in the raveling web of broken threads of thought. Sucking in a deep breath, he held it for a count of ten, willing his muscles to relax, his legs and hands to lose the tension that kept them unconsciously stiff. He went on duty again in five hours, and he would need some rest before then.

The first shooting of that night's tour was reported at 00:28, when Wager and Axton were still at the homicide office going through the last twenty-four hours' circulars and mail. A bar on upper Larimer: three men going out the door bumped into a man coming in, words led to shoves, shoves to a punch or two, and the man ran out to his car and came back with a pistol. By the time the homicide detectives arrived, the uniformed patrol had covered a body with a coarse prison blanket, and an ambulance had taken a second victim to Denver General's emergency room. The third of the trio, beginning to shiver as his shock gave way to awareness of what had exploded around him, gave the officer a description of the assailant. An alert had already gone out in all quarters of the city.

"Pretty cut-and-dried," said Officer Martinez. "We got a couple witnesses who know the dude that was doing all the shooting: Aurelio Rivera. We're trying to get a current address on him now."

Wager nodded and scanned Martinez's notebook, with its list of witnesses and addresses. If shootings had to happen, and they happened so often that necessity seemed a part of it, then he was glad when they were this way: positive identification and enough witnesses to give even Prosecuting Attorney Kolagny a case, and the public defender anxiety hives. "Okay, Marty—good work. We'll take it from here."

The second call came about forty-five minutes later, a

liquor store holdup and a shoot-out between the clerk and the robber. One man dead.

"You want to finish up here?" Wager asked Max.

"Right. Take the car—I'll get a patrol to give me a ride over when I'm through."

As Wager arrived, Lincoln Jones was still flashing his strobe light over the sprawled body, and the ambulance attendants were rolling a squeaking gurney through the propped door. Police-reporter Gargan had his ear hanging over an officer's shoulder to note down what an excited, slab-faced man was saying. The policeman, wide, black face shining with sweat in the warm night air, printed laboriously on a long blue and white form.

Taking a minute to overcome his dislike, Gargan nodded and asked Wager if there was anything new on the killer-angels case.

"No," said Wager. ' Ask Doyle tomorrow."

"It's a big story, Wager. National coverage. If you give me the inside dope I promise I'll hold it until the story breaks. And despite what I think of you, I'll give you a good write-up. You, Doyle, the whole division. You people could use it."

"I'm on a call, Gargan. Talk to Doyle." Wager pushed past him to the black officer and said, "Hello, John. What's the story?"

"Gabe! I was hoping you'd get on over here. This here's Mr. Coleman; he's the clerk. That there's the stick-up man; he's dead. Whyn't you tell your story to Detective Wager, Mr. Coleman? Ain't no sense you having to tell it more'n once."

"Any other witnesses?"

"Nope." Officer Blainey noted on his report that Detective Wager assumed control of the case, and then he capped his Bic pen with a relieved stab.

"Weapons? Dispatcher said shots were exchanged."

"The victim's still got it. He's lying on it." Blainey's face opened in a wide grin. "See you on the street, Gabe."

"Okay, John." Wager, feet beginning to burn, hoisted himself up to sit on the counter beside the cash register. He pulled out his own notebook, dated a page, and jotted down the time and location. Gargan moved a little closer and pretended that Wager wasn't Wager. The pungent smell of cheap bourbon came from half a dozen shattered bottles on the floor behind the counter. Beside the doorway, where the ambulance attendants swerved the wheeled cart out to the curb, a couple of kids breaking the city curfew poked fingers at the bullet hole punched through the plate glass and gazed with wide eyes at the sheeted corpse.

"All right, Mr. Coleman, can I have your full name and home address, please?"

"The sonofabitch came in and pulled a gun, Officer. It was self-defense. He came in and looked around a little and then he came over here and lifted out that pistol from his belt and he said, 'You know what to do—empty it out.' "

"Yessir, we'll get to that in a minute. Can I have your full name and home address, please?"

By the time Wager went off duty he still had not heard from Winston. He placed another call to Loma Vista and a worried voice answered after half a ring, "Yes?"

"Mrs. Winston?"

"Yes . . . yes it is."

"This is Gabe Wager again. Can I talk to Orrin, please?"

"He's not here. He didn't come home last night and I'm worried sick. I thought you might be the sheriff's office. I called them. Orrin's never done this before and I'm worried sick something happened on one of them roads."

Wager heard the edge of hysteria in her voice. "Maybe his truck broke down, Mrs. Winston. He wouldn't try walking, and there's no phone out there. He's probably waiting in his truck until somebody comes along."

"I know, I know. That's what Sheriff Tice said, too. And that Orrin's CB might not work out there. But he's sent somebody out there to look. I thought you were him calling."

"I'm sure it will be all right, ma'am." He wasn't, but that was the polite thing to say.

And she took it that way. "Yes, yes. I'm sure it will. I'll tell him you called when he gets home."

He took the large elevator to Records, turning over in his mind any possible reason why Winston might disappear. There was a lot about the man Wager didn't know, and newsmen sometimes made enemies that had nothing at all to do with avenging angels. If you were like Gargan you could have a whole raft of enemies by simply showing your face. But Gargan hadn't been going out to visit his half-brother to talk about the avenging angels. And Gargan hadn't tried to call Wager with some important message before he disappeared.

When Jo saw him at the counter, she smiled good morning as if they had not had that fumbling, ill-defined argument that was as painful for its lack of focus as it was for its hurt feelings. "Busy night? You look like you could use some coffee."

"The usual summertime crap—bar shootings, holdups." His stomach clenched at the thought of one more acid-filled cup. "But no coffee. Any more and I'll start acting like Munn."

"How's he doing?"

"Don't ask; he might tell you. How about giving me a call when you get off work? I owe you a dinner from last night."

"I'll give you a call. But you don't owe me anything, Gabe. I thought it over, and maybe I was feeling that way —that you owed me something." She fell silent as another policewoman said, "Excuse me," and pulled a form from a drawer behind the counter. "You don't. What I've done has been because I wanted to, and that's all. Maybe," she smiled wryly, "us Italianas just can't help thinking marriage—our Catholic training and *molti bambini.*"

Wager wasn't all that certain he didn't want to owe her something. But he didn't think it was marriage. Not yet, anyway. "Okay. Let's say I want to take you to dinner. For my own selfish reasons."

"You got a date, copper."

He had to break it. He barely remembered to call Jo just after he finished packing and was on his way out the door to Stapleton airport and the small airline that had just opened service between Denver, Loma Vista, and other oil-shale areas on the Western Slope.

In the groggy heat of midafternoon, the telephone had rung him half awake, and the message relayed by Doyle's secretary from Sheriff Tice brought Wager the rest of the way: Orrin Winston had been found shot to death in his pickup truck. The sketch of an avenging angel was tucked between his fingers.

Tice was waiting in front of the small metal building that served as control tower, facility offices, and lobby. Wager, handed his bag as he stepped down the short ladder of the two-engined craft, raised a hand in greeting. With one finger, the sheriff touched the brim of his Stetson in return.

"My car's over here. I got you a room at the Mesaland again."

"Fine. What happened?"

Tice patted a red bandanna at his face as he led Wager to a blue and white Bronco with the sheriff's silver star gleaming on its side. "Hottest damn day of the damn year. Ain't cooling off none, either." He waited until they had driven around the prefabricated metal building and past signs saying ABSOLUTELY NO ADMITTANCE before telling the story. At Mrs. Winston's request, Tice sent Deputy Hodges over to the benchland to see if Orrin was in trouble. "Earl hadn't been out that way in a couple weeks, anyhow," Tice said, excusing more to himself than to Wager the additional drain on the gasoline budget. "He got nine and a half miles out and found the truck and Orrin in it. Shot twice. With a rifle, I reckon. The coroner's sending the bullets over to the CBI lab for identification, but they look to me like .30-30 slugs. One hit him in the front of the left shoulder—that would be the first shot, my guess is—the second just at the throat when he was turned toward the window. It came out the back of his neck and lodged in the seatback." The Stetson bobbed decisively. "Two quick shots at a moving target. It took a pretty good man to do that with a lever-action rifle."

"Fired from the side? The driver's side?"

"Left front. One bullet went through the windshield. Hodges and me searched all over that damn desert and we didn't find any brass."

Wager tried to picture the long shelves of rock and sand and emptiness that Winston had been driving through. "What time do you think he was killed?"

"I reckon about five or six yesterday evening. The coroner's report's not in yet."

"The truck was headed back this way?"

"That's right." Tice's eyes swiveled in their net of wrinkles toward Wager. "You got an idea where he'd been?"

"I asked him to go talk to Zenas Winston."

"I see. He didn't tell his wife that. Just said he was going over to the benchland. That was all he told anybody at the paper, too."

They fell silent in their own thoughts as the sheriff guided the Bronco through the early evening automobiles caught by the town's sluggish traffic lights. He pulled into the parking lot of the Mesaland Motel and shut off the hot motor. Neither man got out yet.

"The benchland's a big place," Wager mused.

"God-awful big," said Tice. "Somebody either knew where he was going, or they followed him."

In the street behind them, a tractor-trailer rapped its exhaust loudly as it geared down for the red light. "You found the avenging angel stuck between his fingers?" Wager asked.

"Left hand. Just like Mueller. Folded over and slid in. Killer probably reached in through the driver's window. No fingerprints anywhere—I dusted it myself. Not a print on it that wasn't Orrin's."

"The picture was the same?"

"Xerox copy." He nodded.

"Any footprints? Any leading up to the car?"

"We looked, Wager. But I reckon somebody dragged the ground and then the wind did the rest. Hodges didn't find him until about noon today. Same thing goes for tire tracks. We found the place where the killer probably waited, but there were no clear tracks. Too sandy."

"I suppose it's too late to drive out for a look."

"It is. Be dusk by the time we got there. We marked the spot with a stake, though, before we brought his truck back. Tell me." Tice's pale-gray eyes settled on Wager again. "What was it you wanted Orrin to talk to Zenas about?"

"To ask if he had any idea where the Kruse family might be hiding."

Tice grunted. Then he asked, "How much do you know about Zenas?"

"He's one of the people you don't want to bother for a little thing like bigamy."

"That's right. His people been here since before Colorado was a state. They stay by themselves over there. Always have. I sort of think of them like Indians on their own reservation."

"That's fine with me."

"It would be just the same if it wasn't fine with you. Now, what makes you think Zenas might know about the Kruses?"

"He kept in touch with Beauchamp. He sent a warning to Kruse through Beauchamp that Willis was looking for them."

"And if the Kruses were running, they might run to Zenas as a friend—I see. Well, Zenas might know something at that." He lifted his Stetson and dragged the bandanna across the red line it left on his forehead. "Those people don't trust strangers, but they got to trust each other. Most of the time, anyway." Then, "You think the avenging angels are still after the Kruse family? Is that it?"

"Yes. And I think we'd better find the Kruses before they do."

Again Tice nodded. "First thing in the morning, I'll have a vehicle ready for you. And a map. I ain't got the time to go with you—commissioners' meeting, budget hearing. But you can drive out to where Orrin was found, then on over to talk to Zenas. I reckon you'll want to do that."

Wager did, but some certainty in Tice's voice made him ask, "Why?"

"Orrin lived long enough to write a couple words: 'water' and 'Wager.' Newspaperman," Tice explained. "Always carried a pencil and paper."

"Water and my name?"

"Yep. The first, I reckon, because he was in that desert and pumping out a lot of blood. The second because he had something for you. Maybe something he found out from Zenas, and Zenas might tell you now."

Before Wager drove off with one of the county's two yellow rescue vehicles, Sheriff Tice jotted down the mileage. "I got to bill that special task force of yours for the gas," he said. "I told that to your man Doyle when I called yesterday."

Wager bet his man Doyle was happy about that. "You say it's a stake with a red cloth tied to it?"

"It marks the left front wheel. Here's a sketch where I figure the sniper stationed himself. This wash, here—you'll see it." Tice handed Wager a carefully drawn sheet of graph paper. "Now, you got extra water in this vehicle, and a radio into our county net. But that don't always work out there—there's a lot of dead spots and skips once you're on the benches. If you get in trouble, don't start walking in that desert. Just stay with the vehicle—it's a lot easier to see than a man, and sooner or later somebody's bound to come along."

"Any reason why I should get in trouble?"

"It's the desert, Wager. Only a damn fool wouldn't be ready for trouble."

The sand road's descent cut through the white glare ahead of him. If he did need the help Tice warned about, Wager hoped it would come sooner rather than later. Without enough water, without shade, without protection from a wind as hot and dry and steady as a sigh from hell, a man might last one day in the sun. Night would bring relief from the heat but not from the thirst. Dawn would bring a flaming sky and the knowledge that he would not live to see sunset.

Between the two worn front seats of the Jeep, a receiver crackled and muttered as distant transmissions ruffled the band. But as soon as Wager dropped over the mesa's edge the radio began to blank into total silence and the only reason now for leaving it on was that even the occasional static was better than hearing nothing but the rush of empty wind.

The last time he had driven this road had been with Orrin. Now the man's torn body lay at the funeral home, where Tice had shown Wager the holes, and the bloodless lips still twisted from the impact of bullets and the effort to write those two last words.

"He must have died pretty quick."

"Emory said maybe two minutes. Either bled to death or drowned in his own blood—throat wound."

"Emory?"

"Emory Wright—funeral director. He's the county coroner."

That was why Tice was satisfied with an either/or cause of death. "Where'd you find Orrin's note?"

"On the floor." Tice showed Wager the man's wire-bound notebook. The tan paper cover was scuffed by fresh dirt. Inked on the cover was a date from a couple of days ago followed by a dash. "I reckon the dirt came when Orrin kicked his legs."

"What's this?" Wager pointed to the date.

"Mrs. Winston says that's Orrin's filing system. He dates his notebooks when he starts one; when it's full, he puts another date on it. Then he files them in the order of the dates."

That explained why the pages were mostly empty. Wager read the earlier entries. A couple of leaves were dedicated to a Mr. Angstrom's ninetieth birthday celebration; a sentence was underlined: *"He was fond of saying you should run through life like a rabbit."* There was a note on a local artist who was opening a new show at the gallery—that would be today—featuring a model for the Coors Beer Cowboy and other genuine western scenes. A cryptic "8 p.m. C." Some memos to himself: "Call Ellie for mock-up Frank's ad," "commiss. meetg 9 Fri." And, underlined, *"Wager,"* followed by a local telephone number.

"Do you know this number?"

"Mine," said Tice. "He called us to get a message to you. He wanted you to call him right away."

And Wager had not been there. The last entry in the book, on a dog-eared page, was in handwriting barely resembling the others. Two words sprawled shakily across the pale-blue lines, as if written with closed eyes and measured by a groping thumb. One was at the top of the page, the other near the bottom: "water" and "Wager."

"How's Mrs. Winston now?"

"Doc's give her a sedative and some neighbors are looking after her." Tice pulled the rubber sheet over Orrin's face. "You'll want to see Orrin's last notebooks?"

He did, but that would have to wait for his return from the benchland, and Mrs. Winston's return from exhausted hysteria.

Wager shifted down as the stiffly sprung vehicle jolted across a series of ruts. According to the map sketched by Tice, the site of Winston's murder should be somewhere within the next two- or three-tenths of a mile. Wager slowed and scanned the line of the road, squinting through the heat that already formed shimmering mirages in the distance. There it was—a pale glint of new wood with a dot of shiny red winking at its top: a strip of fluorescent cloth fluttering in the wind. Stopping the Jeep, Wager surveyed the scene from the slight elevation he had. Orrin's truck had been headed this way; the sniper was hidden on the right side of the road. Probably the small gulley that angled off from the road's shoulder just in front of Wager. It wound behind the low, sandy ridge and then roughly parallel to the road. Here a vehicle could swing into the soft sand of that wash. Wager dropped into four-wheel drive and lurched across the ill-defined shoulder and into the sand.

Slower than a walk, the Jeep nosed down the wind-rippled wash, and Wager noted how the fluted dirt walls rose and fell between him and the distant stake. And, beyond, how the empty road, a pale streak through the low desert brush, could be seen clearly for ten miles before it twisted down to the next broad shelf. You would have plenty of time to get ready, would see the wind-flattened plume of dust coming, maybe the white flash of sun on a windshield. You could leave your vehicle somewhere along here, a four-wheel drive—it would have to be that —and wait until you saw Orrin coming. Wager stopped the Jeep behind a shoulder-high rise in the bank and got out, listening for a moment to the hissing whisper of the wind as it skipped among the stiff, low twigs. You would watch the slow approach of the dust, would walk down this wash, its slice of earth hiding both the waiting vehicle and you from Orrin's eyes. Here the soft sand bed twisted back toward the road, following the steepest fall of land. By stretching a bit, Wager could glimpse the stake over the embankment, closer now; and he began to look with a rifleman's eye for the clearest line of fire and the most stable rest for a prone shot. He found it where the gully bent nearest the road and turned sharply away: a high bank whose crumbling, rock-filled face let boots find a grip to scramble up to the edge and see, about a hundred yards distant, the red flutter of tape and a long, level stretch of road leading up to it.

According to the map, Tice also thought this was the spot. Wager lay there a few seconds, gazing down and imagining the approaching truck jouncing along at about thirty miles an hour almost straight toward this spot. You would see Winston's shirt, pale in the cab's shade. The driver's head would be outlined against the back window. A telescopic sight would bring Winston's hot face full into the circle of glass, and the cross hairs would steady with a smooth, gliding motion of the rifle. One hundred yards at an approaching target: not overly difficult if you're any good with a rifle. But not a beginner's shot, either; not one you would want to snap off too quickly. So you might use a sling, scrape a small hole to rest your elbow; long inhale and hold and squeeze gently the way the rifle instructors chanted at boot camp. *Thump.* A quick flip with the lever, rock solidly back into position, and one second later the next round on its way. Two shots, that quick and that tight in the target area—definitely not a beginner, definitely shots with some risk to them. Pick up the spent brass, a single golden tube, still hot but within arm's reach. Down to the skewed truck to make sure.

Wager rose and brushed the sand from his clothes and walked down to the stake. He paused to look back at his line of tracks wavering between brush and rocks. If Orrin had been able to see, the killer would have come straight toward him, a figure squinting against the sun in his face. But far enough away not to be recognized yet—not by a man who had just been shot twice and who, under the stunning impact, knew he was dying fast. Twenty, at most thirty seconds to fumble out the notebook and write those two words. Half again that long to pick up the brass and jog the hundred yards up to the truck window. Probably slow down a step or two away, rifle at port arms just in case, hungry to see the victim totally motionless. Maybe a trifle frightened. Wager hoped so. He would like it if the killer had felt at least a twitch of fear when he leaned into the hot cab of the truck to slip the avenging angel between Winston's still-warm fingers.

He reached Zenas's ranch near midday, and under the numbing weight of noon sun the sandstone building seemed emptier than the last time. No one opened the blank wooden door to welcome him; no piping child's voice carried like the call of far-off birds through the waterfall sound of the cottonwoods. Instead, Wager stood alone on the tiny concrete slab with its embedded colored stones and knocked loudly. When no one answered, he walked around into the cottonwood shade and across the sandy yard toward the barn that dominated the packed earth and rail fences of the animal pens. A quiet voice from behind a screen of pungent mountain willow said "Hello," and Wager, the hairs prickling up his nape, froze.

"You're that Denver policeman." Zenas, a rifle hanging comfortably in the crook of his arm, stood up among the tangle of willow branches. "Where's Orrin at?"

"He's been killed. He was shot two days ago on the way back to Loma Vista."

The man's flat, wide shoulders sagged but his face remained as closed as a fist. "The destroying angels?"

"Yes. Sheriff Tice found a drawing just like the others."

Zenas let his gaze shift from Wager to the yellow Jeep and back up the road to the notch carved like a rifle sight in the wall of red sandstone. "You best come into the trees."

Wager, too, glanced around the etched line of slick rock that towered over this corner of the river bottom. On the first trip, those walls seemed to keep strangers out; now they seemed to gaze inward to pin down any figure standing, like Wager, in plain view of the rim. He stepped quickly into the mottled green of tangled willow; wordless, Zenas led him a few steps along a dim trail to where even the hard blue sky was masked by peppery-smelling leaves.

"You think they know you're here?" Wager asked.

His jaw moved slightly before he spoke, as if the words needed a running start to overcome his dislike of talking to a Gentile. "Willis visited with us before him and Ervil started their fight."

"And he knows that you sided with Ervil?"

"He does."

"Have you had any trouble lately?"

"Not yet."

Wager listened to the high whine of an insect dodging among the pale leaves and veering sharply away from their two motionless figures. "Have you got the Kruse family hidden out here?"

Zenas's dark eyes widened slightly. He was not used to lying; by avoiding Gentiles, he had no pressures to lie. But he didn't have to answer clearly, either. "Why do you ask that?"

"The last time I was here, Willis knew whose side you were on—that's why you had Orrin bring me out here with those pictures. But you weren't worried for yourself then. Now you're worried enough to hide your family somewhere around here, and I think it's because you've done something that Willis wants to get even with you for —taken the Kruse family in, maybe."

"You're a good hunter." But he still wasn't willing to answer directly. "What makes you think my family's nearby?"

"The farm's kept up. Do you and your boys come in and work it nights?"

Zenas sighed. If a stranger and Gentile could figure it out, then so could the destroying angels. "I hoped we wouldn't have to flee our homestead. My family, my children, they haven't seen the ways of . . . of strangers, and I don't wish to lead them into that corruption. But God's will be done; we are his servants."

If everything that happened was God's will, then there was no need for policemen like Wager. But his feeling was that any God there might be didn't care very much anymore what humans did to each other. That left the responsibility with people. "Maybe we ought to help God out a little bit, Mr. Winston. What did you tell Orrin before he started home?"

The word "God" in the mouth of a Gentile was blasphemy. But it was true that he often moved in dark and mysterious ways, and that he helped those who, with a pure heart, helped themselves. "I told him that I knew where the Kruse family lay hidden from the Antichrist, and that they were safe, God willing."

"But you didn't tell him where?"

"He knew better than to ask."

"Well, I've only got the manners of a Gentile—"

"Yea, verily."

"—and of a cop. We are willing to offer protection to the Kruses until this avenging-angel thing is cleared up."

"The protection of Gentiles? To our people?"

"Yes."

Zenas's narrow lips stretched in a bitter smile. "That would be new under the sun. But this 'thing' will live as long as Willis and his followers do. It's part of the eternal war between the Antichrist and the Chosen." He gave his head a firm shake. "Against that, your shield is as clay, your sword as wood."

Despite the thick and close shade they stood in, Wager was hot; he was thirsty from the dry air, which sucked up any sweat as soon as it showed, and his restless sleep at the motel had left him dull and weary when he woke up this morning. Moreover, he was quickly growing tired of biblical phrases which, despite the fixed and glittering eye of a true believer, rang more than once with a note of pretension. "Mr. Winston, we are going to catch the avenging angels. No question about that. But how much more damage they'll do before we catch them, I don't know—and neither do you. The Kruses will be safer with police protection, and if you've been threatened you'll need it, too. If you know where they are, tell me so I can arrange that protection. Otherwise, if anything happens to them it's on your head."

"My responsibility to my people is glory unto God." He shook his head once more. "Good-bye."

"Yeah," said Wager.

For the long ride back, Wager snapped the canvas top into place across the Jeep's metal struts. Already he could feel that crinkly dryness of sunburn on his forehead and cheeks, and the heat gathered from the morning's glare now radiated back from the hot sand and stone to add itself to the burden of the afternoon sun. As he squinted against the desert brightness and half consciously aimed his wheels along the ruts climbing the escarpments, he let his thoughts flow around Orrin's death. He was certain that the Kruses were hiding with Zenas. Orrin had probably been just as sure, but he wrote nothing about it in his notebook. That was something you whispered into one ear only, not something you told the world in writing that might be seen by any pair of eyes. "Wager." Call Wager —Orrin wanted whoever found him to call Denver because Wager was supposed to know something or learn something. Well, Wager knew why he sent Orrin out to see Zenas. And now he knew as much as Orrin about the Kruses. What else? Anything else? What did not fit was why Orrin would be killed. Why would the avenging angels shoot someone like Orrin? A message? A warning to Zenas? Why bother? Zenas knew they were after him, and he was already worried enough to hide his family. Was Orrin killed to keep him from getting to Wager? . . . But Wager could go to the source, too—had gone, for all the good it did. . . .

Eyes heavy from the heat and wind and glare, Wager nudged the hard tires hissing through the deep sand that kicked against the steering wheel. The sniper had fired from concealment. He had hidden his car behind a ridge of earth like any of a dozen Wager could see right now. But suppose he had left it in the open? Why wouldn't Orrin, like anybody else, drive unsuspectingly toward it? Curious, maybe; certainly alert. But there was as yet no sign that the avenging angels were out here on the benchland; Mueller's death had been in those far mountains hidden by distant rimrock. And who would know Orrin had driven out to talk to Zenas? Someone knew, feared, and waited—out of sight of the victim. A hundred yards away from a moving target . . . How much easier it would have been to drive slowly toward Orrin's truck down this rough, one-lane road. Just pull over to let Orrin's laboring vehicle jounce slowly past; wave and smile, and then, with the victim three or four feet away, shoot him with a pistol. Why risk a hundred-yard shot at a moving target? Unless the killer thought Orrin had reason to be afraid and on guard. Maybe in those notebooks . . . Maybe Mrs. Winston would know if Orrin was afraid of someone. A message? Was Orrin's death simply a message like the bloody angel scrawled in Beauchamp's house?

Wager tried to focus his mind on the questions, but no answers came. Just more possibilities that blurred any clear line of cause and effect that he could work back from the fact of Orrin's death. A lurching *thump* sent the Jeep leaning heavily sideways and tossed the sheriff's logbook from the cowl onto the floor. Wager pulled the wheels back into the ruts and bent to pick up the small book.

With a hollow *pop*, sharp jets of glass stung into his neck and cheek and left eye. The windshield splattered over his lap in a crumbling blanket of safety glass and Wager swerved sharply off the road to tilt the car high. Flipping off the ignition as he dived from the low side, he already had his pistol in his fist when he hit the ground flat, eye burning and watering with each blink of the stinging lid.

A second shot hit somewhere on the vehicle and this time Wager heard the weapon, the high-velocity crack of a rifle aimed at him from not too far away. Blinking painfully to see, he crawled behind the ridge at the side of the wheel tracks and cautiously peeked toward the sound of the weapon. A blue puff of smoke thinned rapidly in the strong wind and then he heard the crank of a starter, saw the black line of a whip antenna glide and snap just beyond a rise of land. A moment later, a haze of dust caught in the wind and Wager, standing, trying to glimpse the fleeing car, heard the heavy engine strain away.

His eye. The pain had been there all along, but now,

with the sniper gone, it suddenly throbbed and burned as though acid had been spilled across it. He fumbled a handkerchief out of his back pocket and blotted at the hot and seeping flesh, trying to keep his twitching lid from burying any glass deeper in the eye. Sniper. Just like Orrin. Wager groped for the radio, pressing the Transmit button despite the silence of his speaker. It might work—sometimes you could transmit when you couldn't receive. Orrin had had a CB in his truck. He hadn't had a chance to use it. If Wager hadn't bent down at that moment—he pressed again, calling for Tice, calling for an intercept at the edge of the benchland. Now he could see the plume of dust from the fleeing car glide above a ridge of brush, and he followed the rising cloud of yellow haze as the sniper fled.

Cranking the engine and cursing as it hung fire, he finally coughed it into life and started after the dust cloud, now rising with increasing speed above the rolling earth. But his steering wheel pulled hard left through the sand, and, holding the handkerchief over his burning eye to try to still the pain, he saw that the second shot had torn a large hole in the knobbed tire. Ahead, the dust plume sped away from the crippled Jeep.

Wager again tried the silent radio. No answer, not even a querying crackle of static. He turned off the engine and groped for the water can strapped to the Jeep's side. It was sun-warmed and smelled of metal, but the wet handkerchief cooled his burning eye, and he washed the eye gently with water cupped in his hands to dislodge the chips of glass that clung to his eyeball. Safety glass. But when it shattered under a bullet's impact . . . And if he had not reached for that fallen book . . .

There was still glass in his eye and it felt like scorching lumps of gravel, but there was nothing else he could do.

Soaking his handkerchief again, he tied it gently over the hot lid to try to keep from blinking. Gritting his teeth against the burning sting, Wager began to change the tire. Far ahead, the sniper's car was a dark spot followed by a high yellow tail like a speeding dust devil.

9.

"Hold still."

"I'm trying."

He felt the heat of the lamp against his cheek, and across his clamped-open, drying eye saw the blinding whiteness of the circular mirror. "I thought doctors had stopped wearing those things."

"Not if they need to use both hands. Hold still now."

Wager heard Sheriff Tice come back into the clinic's small examining room behind him, the creak of his pistol belt and his heavy breath loud in the quiet room.

"Did you get her?" Wager asked.

"Please don't talk."

"Yep. She's a lot calmer now. Says we can come over any time and look through whatever we want to." He heard Tice settle into a chair. "I called your man Doyle, too. He wants you to call him as soon's you can. He wants to know if you need medical leave or a replacement."

"No," said Wager.

The doctor breathed "Damnit" and leaned forward again, steel instrument glittering in the white light. "Both you people shut your damn mouths."

They did, the doctor finally squirting a cooling jelly into the corner of Wager's eye and taping a gauze pad lightly over it. "I think I got all the glass, but it'll feel pretty rough for a while. And look a lot rougher when the bandage comes off. Which," he added, washing his hands in the corner sink, "shouldn't happen for twenty-four hours. You should visit an ophthalmologist when you're back in Denver, Detective Wager, just to be sure."

"No permanent damage, is there, Doc?" asked Tice.

"I don't think so—most of it was at the side of the eye-ball. Discoloration and a lot of discomfort. But if it keeps bothering you, or if your vision doesn't clear up a few hours after you take the bandage off, be certain to go to an ophthalmologist."

"Okay."

Tice grunted himself to his feet. "Well, that's good. Doyle seemed to want to blame me for you getting cut up." He led Wager out of the clinic toward the parking lot. "Hell, I told him he wouldn't have to pay for the windshield. We got comprehensive insurance for things like that."

"Doyle always sounds like he's chewing somebody out for something," said Wager. "That's just his way."

"Well, I wondered at the time about sending you out there alone. But with only two deputies for the whole damn county . . ." He added, just loudly enough for Wager to hear, "And anyway, if a man wears a badge he should be able to take care of himself."

"I can," said Wager. "And I did. It wasn't your fault—it's whoever took a shot at me." It was the fault of whoever saw Wager go out there as Orrin had; whoever knew what kind of vehicle he would be driving and about what time he would be coming back. "But, Sheriff, I do think the case security might be tighter."

"Security?" He turned over Wager's meaning as he

keyed the ignition. "Oh—I see. By damn, that's something I hadn't even got to thinking about yet. But you're right. Absolutely. Somebody had to know when and where you were going." The Bronco pulled onto the highway. "Trouble is, that could be half the county. I radioed in the request for a vehicle for you last night; told them you'd be in to pick it up this morning. Every son of a gun with a police scanner —and that's almost everybody—heard the request."

"Why so many scanners?"

"Nosiness, I guess. People leave them on all day and night. Like listening in on a party line. Hell," he said, "half the county knew why you were coming before you got here. The other half knows now."

He handed Wager a thin newspaper whose ink tended to smear. In some kind of ornate gothic script, the banner read LOMA VISTA MORNING STAR, and beneath it in square, solid black print was LOCAL EDITOR SLAIN. The story was a long one, covering most of the front page and complete with photographs of Orrin as a smiling young man, an older Orrin with his bolo tie, shaking hands with somebody wearing a dignified suit, and finally Orrin being carried in under a sheet. The reporter had envisioned his story being picked up by the news wires and had given it every angle of coverage he could think of.

"You're mentioned down there."

A short paragraph called Wager a homicide specialist from Denver and said he was part of a statewide team investigating an outbreak of killer-angel murders such as the still-unsolved shooting of Frederick Mueller of Rio Piedra and the slaughter of a family in Denver. It could have been worse; the story could have had his photograph and itinerary—except that whoever shot at him already knew that.

"I reckon it was the same one who shot Orrin," said Tice.

"Same m.o., anyway. Where did Orrin file those notebooks?"

"I didn't ask. Nelly'll tell us."

"When you talked to her," Wager asked quietly, "was she home alone?"

It took a couple of seconds, but without another word Sheriff Tice flipped on his lights and siren and the Bronco surged forward with a heavy whine as he floored the gas pedal.

Because he, like Wager, figured that someone had shot Orrin because the editor knew something incriminating; he shot at Wager because he was afraid he might have learned it. Now he might believe that Orrin had told his wife.

In a swirl of dust and barking dogs, Tice braked the vehicle in front of a frame house in the middle of a large lot beyond the edge of town. Through the fading light, Wager could see a small orchard of whitewashed fruit trees, a grape arbor near the house's porte cochere, the peak of a small barn over the roof line, where a mercury vapor light was just beginning to glow a weak purple. The silhouette of a woman stood against the lighted doorway and peered out at the commotion. Tice reached the porch even before Wager. "Hello, Ruth—I'm glad you're here. How's Nelly?"

The woman, thin as a rake handle and with as many curves, held open the screen door and said "Hush" to the still-yapping dogs. "Hush, now! Git!" Then to Tice, her gaze catching the white patch over Wager's eye, "She's holding up. I heard you-all coming a half-mile away."

"Oh, just trying out my equipment," said Tice. "Nobody's been around?"

"Around?"

"Reporters. Nosy neighbors. Anybody."

"No, everybody's been real thoughtful." She led the two

men into a parlor that centered around a large fieldstone fireplace. On the mantel were family pictures in a row; against one wall, a glass-faced cabinet tilted up some flowered dishes for people to see. Mrs. Winston rose from a wingback chair to say hello. She had a powdery-looking face and her gray hair was braided up over her ears in an old-fashioned way. Her eyes, behind rimless bifocals, were baggy from crying; but now she smiled, and in that smile Wager could see the girl Winston had married.

"Hello, D.L. And this is Detective Wager? I'm pleased to meet you. Orrin had good things to say about you."

Wager had barely known Orrin and hadn't spent much time at all thinking about him, until after he was dead. "Thank you, ma'am. I'm sorry about what happened."

The smile quivered but did not break. "Yes," she said.

"We won't stay long, Nelly. You understand. But we'd like to see the notebooks you told us about."

"They're at the office." She went to a small side table and took a ring of keys out of the drawer. Holding them a moment, she fingered the stone that hung like a fob. Wager saw the blue tint of turquoise, matching the slide that Orrin wore on his tie. "This," she held up a brass key, "is the front door. This one is for his office. This little one's the cabinet. Orrin kept the notebooks in the cabinet behind his desk."

"We won't disturb nothing," said Tice.

She patted his hand as if it were he who needed sympathy. "Nobody can disturb anything now."

"Ruth'll stay with her until the kids get in for the funeral." Tice steered the Bronco back toward town and the newspaper office. "I don't think an avenging angel's going to try something with other people around. And with those dogs.

But I'll have Hodges cruise the area anyway—he can keep an eye on the women without scaring them to death."

Wager remembered the line of bodies carried out of the Beauchamp house. "I hope that's so."

"You don't think it is?"

"They've killed men, women, and children. And they're not through killing yet if we don't catch them."

"Goddamnit, Wager, I'm doing the best I can to catch them!"

"Me, too. And so far that's not much, is it?"

They drove in silence down the long, rectilinear dirt roads that carved the flat land into large, square lots. Out of the dark on either side came the pale-blue glow of mercury lamps over barns, or the yellow of windows in flat-roofed houses and mobile homes moored like boxcars among the sagebrush. Wager watched the approaching glow of traffic along the highway until they finally turned off Main Street onto Third, stopping in front of a single-story brick building painted white. No light shone through the plate-glass windows but, catching the weak gleam of a street lamp high on a telephone pole, a gilded sign spelled GRANT COUNTY BEACON—THE COUNTY'S ONLY NEWSPAPER. A smaller sign taped on the door said OFFICE CLOSED BECAUSE OF DEATH. Tice radioed his location and the code that said he would be temporarily out of the net. Then he unlocked the front door.

It swung into a small room cluttered with the paper debris of news work that is forever unfinished and hurried. Even a weekly seemed to have deadline troubles, and, Wager guessed, reporters were alike everywhere in dumping their sheets and galleys on any ledge and for no apparent reason.

Tice fumbled along the inside wall for a light switch, found it, and flooded the room in the antiseptic glare of fluorescent light. "This is Orrin's office back here."

He led Wager between the cluttered desks and work tables smelling of rubber cement to a door whose frosted glass panel loomed darkly. When he flipped on the light, the sheriff said "Damn" and Wager, following his gaze, saw it too: the alley window had a pane taped over and smashed out; the sash hung half open. The clutter of this room was not the orderly chaos of the outer office, but a scattering of paper and printed sheets that someone had ripped through in a hurried search.

"How's the cabinet?"

Tice, wrapping the bandanna around his hand, pressed the very end of the handle. "Still locked."

Wager pointed to a ripple in the lip of the metal door. A glint showed where the paint had freshly chipped. "Someone was trying to pry it open. I think we scared them off."

Tice wheeled and lumbered toward the front door, the handle of his pistol snagging one of the tables with a scraping *thump.* Outside, they listened for a moment to the darkness.

"You go that way—take the alley. I'll meet you around back."

Wager turned into the narrow lane between the newspaper office and the neighboring building. In the thick darkness, his shoes snagged on grass clumps and kicked against whiskey bottles; ahead, a pale rectangle, the alley ended in a sandy lane empty of everything except wind-blown trash and clusters of garbage cans that looked like crouching figures. A moment later, Tice's squat shadow turned the far corner toward Wager.

"Nothing?"

"No," said Wager. "He must have heard us at the front door."

"Damn," said Tice.

Back in Orrin's rifled office, Wager inspected the windowsill while Tice jiggled the key in the bent locker door. Splintered glass hung at the ends of the masking tape, and a fresh dent showed where a screwdriver had been used to pry open the sash. Whoever broke in apparently did not know exactly what to look for or where, and had spent a lot of time fumbling through desk drawers and piles of paper before turning to the cabinet. But another two or three minutes with that thin metal and the intruder might have found what he was looking for. Wager and Tice could thank the gods of luck for a little help.

"There," said Tice. The cabinet door snapped open with a *twang*. He rummaged for a moment and then told a hovering Wager, "They're still here." Carefully, he lifted out a handful of cardboard filing boxes and carried them to the littered desk. Then, using the bandanna again, Tice picked up the telephone and dialed his office. "Joanne? D.L. here. See if you can get me that fingerprint kit. Anybody that's around, have them bring it over to the *Beacon*'s office. He is? What for? All right, have him bring it over." As he hung up, he told Wager, "Yates is in town for some paperwork—he'll bring it over."

The spiral notebooks had been placed in cardboard file boxes lined in marbled gray and white sides. Dates inked on white paper had been glued to the black spines of the boxes. Wager pulled out the most recent, scanning the pages for any mention of the avenging angels. Tice, after a quick prowl of the room, hung over his shoulder and breathed heavily in the still office.

"Anything?"

"Not yet." The entries quickly became routine; Orrin began a section with a list of meetings for that week—city council, PTA, county board—and, a few pages later, there were his notes on the meetings. The items between were the usual ones, and they were often in cryptic abbreviations, some of which Wager could decipher. Perhaps Orrin's wife could do the rest. Or, better, one of the newspaper staff.

"Do you know who 'C' is?"

Tice grunted no. "But he wrote down a meeting with 'C' in his last notebook, didn't he?"

That was the point; Wager didn't bother to answer.

They finished that notebook and were halfway into the next when a knock rattled the front door loudly. Tice went and a moment later came back followed by Deputy Yates, who carried a metal tool kit. On its lid was stenciled FIN-GERPRINT KIT COUNTY SHERIFF. Yates peered at Wager. "What in hell happened to your eye?"

"I got some glass in it."

The deputy winced. "Man, just the thought of that's like sand between my teeth!" He shuddered and lugged the kit to the half-open window. "This here's the spot?"

"Start there," said Tice. "Then the cabinet and the handles."

"Right." He, too, glanced over Wager's shoulder at the notebooks. "You found them in the cabinet? Anything there?"

Wager shook his head. "Nothing I can find."

"No avenging angels?"

"No."

By the time Yates had finished dusting for prints, Wager and Tice had read a year's collection of notebooks. In the one covering Mueller's death they found the only mention of avenging angels. The rest held now-familiar phrases and memos, and names that began to echo periodically as Orrin noted his rounds and appointments. Wager's good eye watered from the strain of doing all the work, and he rubbed at it wearily. "It's got to be in these last couple notebooks," he said to himself.

But Tice answered. "If there's anything there at all. Damned if I think there's anything there at all. What about you, Roy? You come up with any prints?"

The deputy shook his head. "That sill's clean of everything. I'd say it was wiped off. Or the guy wore gloves. There's some prints on that cabinet handle, but they're pretty dry. That means they're old," he added, to impress Wager with his skill.

But Wager's attention was elsewhere, and the remark went past him. Orrin had been killed because someone thought he knew something; Wager had been shot at for the same reason; now a burglary had been attempted for those notebooks, which were supposed to tell them something. But no recent mention of avenging angels, no name or place or time linked to that group of murderers who loomed so threateningly over Orrin's half-brother and ultimately over Orrin himself. It just didn't make sense. "I'd like to make copies of these last two or three books, Sheriff. Maybe somebody else will see something that I don't."

"All right by me," said Tice. "You through, Roy? Let's take one more look outside then. Get your flashlight."

They made a final sweep of the alley, using the headlights of Tice's Bronco and the sharp gleam of flashlights to pick out any fresh tracks. But the dirt was scuffed only by blurred footprints, new and old, and nowhere did a line of crushed weeds or ridged sand clearly indicate the wheels of a vehicle. Yates, his long-handled flashlight sweeping back and forth, finally spotted some fresh ruts in the sand at the rear of the building. "This must be where he parked. But you're not going to get any impressions in this loose crap."

That was true. And in fact the whole damn case seemed like loose sand to Wager. Nothing stuck together; it all slid apart and trickled between his fingers. Into this surrounding darkness the burglar had run; perhaps out of it, as near as a touch, the killer would come again. Yet no matter how hard Wager tried, he could not pull things together into a pattern of cause and effect. It brought the kind of feeling he hated most, a sense that no matter how hard he tried he would not be able to grasp that pattern. But the pattern had to be there. And the fact that he was too blind to spot it made its absence sting all the more.

He was tired. Although he had slept heavily, the night had seemed as brief as a wink, and Wager was still tired when he rolled out of bed in the morning. The day before had been a very long one; it always did things to your sense of time when somebody shot at you. When the last surge of adrenaline finally ebbed, it left a sense of collapse at the center of the brain where effort came from. He had discovered that in Vietnam, and it was true now. But a shower would help; that, a careful unpeeling of the bandage from his gummy eye, and a squirt of the cooling ointment given him by the doctor. The ball was bright red with irritation and flecked with dark blood, and tears washed out of the corner of his eye when the light stabbed at the soreness. Wash carefully, try to keep from scratching the itchy feeling, retape with a fresh pad. Shave, breakfast the specialty of the house—huevos rancheros, but don't touch those hash browns—and then back to his room to wrestle once more with the heavy sheets of paper onto which they had Xeroxed the pages of Orrin's notebooks.

Taking each entry and numbering it, Wager gradually worked up a classification system—civic meetings, production memoranda, obvious news items, names of assorted people, and, most important: questionable. As he fit an entry under a heading he penciled a light X on the notebook page beside it. Gradually the sifting left fewer and fewer items without an X, but those that remained gained in importance. At least they would look interesting until somebody could explain them away, because they were the "questionable" items.

That phase of the process would take legwork; but just as he was leaving his telephone rang and Jo's worried voice was at his ear, asking him how he was, how badly he was hurt.

"I'm all right. It was only some glass in my eye, but the doctor got it out. It feels better already," he said, lying.

"I was so worried. Max just came by and told me. He said you were okay, but I was so scared. I guess I still am."

At the time, Wager had been more startled and angry and very, very alert than frightened; now that it was over and death had missed him, there wasn't much sense in dwelling on it. "I really am all right, Jo. How about you— how're you doing?"

"Oh, Gabe!" Her voice pulled away with a sigh and a moment later came back half humorously. "You won't even let me worry about you, will you?"

"Jo, there's not one damn thing—"

"I know. But I'm still glad you're all right. I've got to get back on duty—will you give me a call as soon as you get home?"

"I'll do more than that. We've still got that dinner date."

"I'm waiting." Her voice said that she, too, knew how unsatisfactory telephones were. "Oh . . . we missed Polly's barbecue . . . you were down in Pueblo. I told Max we were sorry. Both of us."

Wager wasn't sorry. "That's nice. I forgot all about the damn thing."

"I know. Gabe, please be careful!"

"Well, sure!" That was a silly thing to tell him. "And you be good."

"That's a silly thing to say. Bye."

The buzz of the telephone line seemed almost mocking.

He began the second stage of the process by driving the yellow Jeep with its shattered windshield folded down through the tourist traffic to the *Beacon*'s office. The CLOSED sign was still hanging, but the door stood open to the street, where a few people walked slowly along narrow sidewalks that were already searing hot.

Wager stood in the empty outer office until a woman, face drawn with concentration, came out of Orrin's room. "Oh! Sorry, we're not open for business. I'm just here cleaning up some things."

He showed his badge. "Is anything missing from the break-in?"

"It doesn't look like it. But they certainly made a mess. If Orrin had seen it . . ."

She was in her early thirties, dark hair showing an occasional glint of gray. Her name was Claire Lewis. Mrs. Claire Lewis. "Are you the 'C' that Orrin put down in his notebooks?"

"The 'C'?"

"Yes, ma'am. I'm trying to learn if anything in his notebooks can give a reason why somebody would shoot him." He lay a sheet on the counter for her to look at. "Did you meet with him at eight last Tuesday evening?"

"Tuesday? Yes—that's budget night. I do the books," she explained. "It's one of the things I do, anyway. We meet every Tuesday night at the Mesaland bar to go over the advertising accounts. Orrin said he could never look at an account book without a beer in his hand." She smiled. "He never did, either."

"At eight o'clock at night?"

"Yes. The paper goes to bed around six or seven on Tuesdays. Then we go over the books for an hour or two and then Orrin picks up the first run around nine or ten." She corrected her tense, "Picked up. We distribute on Wednesday morning," she added softly.

"I see." He made a little note beside that entry on the sheet. "Everybody liked Orrin?"

"They did. And I can't think of many people in the world he didn't like. Certainly no one who would do such a terrible thing. Poor Nelly."

"He had no enemies at all?"

"No. This," her palm swung around the office, "was a labor of love as much as a business for him. He said it gave him a chance to meet the people of the county and introduce them to each other. He'd joke about getting paid to be nosy, but he really was serious about the feeling of community that the paper developed. Birthdays, high school graduations, communions, obituaries—they weren't just vital statistics for him; they were stories about his friends. And he'd always leave room in the newshole for what he called the happy stories—births, an anniversary celebration, the kinds of things that get buried in the back pages of the daily." She scratched some pencil lines on a sheet of newsprint. "Maybe that sounds corny to you, but Orrin believed that those were the most important stories."

"He did a lot of the reporting himself?"

"He had to. I have the women's page—club news, weddings. And Ida Jenkins has the school and church news. But other than that, the stories were generally Orrin's. The local ones. National and state we get off the wire."

Ida Jenkins. That would be the "I" Winston had noted

here and there. Wager jotted that down, his satisfaction at defining another unknown mixed with the frustration of learning its unimportance. "Did he ever get into anything controversial?"

"Of course. Orrin loved the town council meetings. And if you think a small town doesn't have room for controversy, well . . ." She ran out of words to illustrate with. "But that was part of what Orrin liked about Grant County. He said that even the worst of the lot were honest in their greed. He said he could forgive anything but phoniness, and he didn't find much of that around here."

"Not even," Wager asked, "with the avenging angels?"

Mrs. Lewis frowned and watched a figure stroll slowly across the street in the white glare. "I've heard stories. I'm not Mormon myself, but everybody's heard stories. And you know that Orrin comes from a Mormon background—so far back it could never catch up, he used to say."

"Yes."

Her mouth tightened. "You know about his relatives over on the benchland? The ones who belong to that splinter church?"

"Orrin told me about them."

"Well, if anybody knows anything about avenging angels, I think it would be them."

"You don't like them?"

"I don't know them and I don't want to. They have primitive and demeaning practices. But I suppose they have a right to live life as they see fit. As long as they stay over there. I cannot understand any woman tolerating that, though."

"So you don't believe in the avenging angels?"

She paused again, a worried wrinkle coming over her nose. "I didn't think so. But those horrible murders in Denver. And then Mueller. And now poor Orrin. But why? Why would anyone—avenging angels or anyone—want to kill Orrin?"

Wager had asked that a few times, too, and had come up with the same answer: "I don't know."

"Of course you don't. That's why you're here, isn't it?"

"Yes, ma'am. Orrin didn't tell you why he was going to the benchland three days ago?"

"Has it only been that long?" She looked around the office. "It seems like a week already. No, he didn't tell me or Ida anything except that he was going over there. Which isn't unusual; he chased stories all over the county—we're the only countywide paper. Sometimes he would tell us what he was working on, other times he wouldn't. He'd just leave a note saying when he'd be back. If we needed him we could usually raise him on the CB." She gestured toward a small transmitter resting on top of a filing cabinet.

"Did he leave a note that day?"

"No, he just said, 'See you tomorrow.' "

But someone had to know so they could dry-gulch him. "Did he seem at all worried or excited or different in any way before he left?"

"No . . . Well, maybe . . . I mean it wasn't a jumping-up-and-down kind of excitement, but he did have this kind of gleam in his eyes when he was on to a good story or when he was telling a joke. He was that way all morning just before he left, and I think it had something to do with you. He came in late—which isn't unusual; it was distribution day, and things are slow that day. I handle distribution, too, so any glitches are mine. But he was very anxious to hear from you, I remember that. He even called the sheriff's office a couple times to see if they were in touch with you yet."

"But he didn't give you any idea what it was about?"

"Oh, no—he was a newsman. He wouldn't talk a story out until it was down on paper."

"Would you look at some of these notebook entries? I think I've figured out most of them, but there's a few that are still puzzling. Like who 'C.H.' might be."

"C.H.?" She wagged her head. "I don't know any C.H."

He pointed to the entry on the page. It read "C.H. ck recs" and was bracketed by Wager's red pencil.

"Oh, maybe it's 'courthouse.' Sometimes he used C.H. for courthouse. It means he wanted to go by the courthouse to check on some kind of records."

"But you don't know what kind?"

"No. It's one of his story-notes."

"How about this series of numbers?" He pointed farther down the page.

"I have no idea at all. I don't think it has anything to do with the paper."

She read further. There were five more obscure entries, two of which she cleared up: "This is a garage appointment. He was always late getting that truck tuned for spring."

"This is summer."

"I said he was always late." She pointed to another bracketed note. "This is a leather shop. They owe us for three months' ads, and he was supposed to go by and talk to them."

"Do you carry delinquent accounts that long?"

"Oh, sure. It's a seasonal business. And advertisers are hard to find for a weekly."

"But nobody owed Orrin a lot of money?"

"Do you mean enough to shoot him for? No, nobody around here has a lot of money to owe. Most of us work for extra cash, but we live off our farms or ranches. We're not as bad as the northern part of the county, but we can still show you some fine examples of rural poverty. You people in Denver," her mouth tightened again, "you've got the votes so you get the government handouts. But out here, if we don't look after ourselves nobody looks after us." She added, "We like it that way."

The city folks sang a different tune, but Wager just nodded and tried to get Mrs. Lewis back to the notebooks. "This one here?"

"I have no idea. It looks like 'Why with above in sheriff's office.' S.O. usually means sheriff's office, but it could be a name."

It wasn't all loss. Wager thanked her and took a few minutes in the Jeep to jot down the translations. Then he headed for the next stop, the courthouse.

"Orrin Winston." The old man scratched under his chin with ink-stained fingers. "Poor Orrin—that was quite a shock. Quite a shock indeed."

"Yessir. I wonder if he came in to check any of your records about three or four days ago."

"They're my records, all right. Ain't nobody else knows the filing system—hee. Ain't many folks come down here, either—law clerks, mostly, and they don't like to talk, just snoop-snoop-snoop and then leave without even a thank-you. Deputies are all right. Once in a while a deputy comes by to talk some. And Orrin now and then. But mostly he spent his time up in Vital Statistics. They're upstairs."

"I've just come from there." And from the court records and from the health records and from election and voter records and from motor vehicle records. Every division of the county government seemed to have its own records office buried away on different floors and in different wings of the old brownstone building. Periodic remodeling had changed the interior and lightened it a bit, but the wide stairways still smelled of aging wood and decades of dust, and the echoes generated beneath the towering silver-painted dome caused a sad, unending murmur all over the building. Now he stood in the cool of a subbasement room, whose door said PROPERTY AND LAND RECORDS, and faced this white-haired man whose skin was the color of potato shoots. "Well, they're my records all right. How old you think I am?"

"How old?"

"How old? How old?"

He looked maybe a hundred and twenty. "Sixty?"

"Hee! Fool them every time. Seventy-seven last October. Going on seventy-eight. And they can't fire me because I'm the only one knows the filing system!"

"That's mighty nice. Did Orrin come in a few days ago?"

"Yes! I told you that. Usually he went up to Vital Statistics and spent his time there. Didn't come down here to see me much. Too busy, he claimed. But I don't believe a word of it. I seen work in my seventy-seven years, young man, and there wasn't none of it sticking to Orrin."

"Yessir. Can you tell me what he was after when he came in?"

"My records! That's what they're all after. You too, right?"

"Yessir. The same ones Orrin looked at."

"The same ones? All of them?"

"Did he look at a lot?"

"Three whole books. Spent half a day right at that table looking through three books of transfers. Thought I was going to have to charge him rent. Hee-hee—get it? Charge him rent because he used the table so long."

"Yessir." Wager thumbed through the sheets of Orrin's notes and laid one on the counter. He pointed to the series of numbers. "Is this some kind of index to your records?"

"Let me see." The old man pulled out a rectangular magnifying glass and held it above the entry, lips moving as he read. "Could be—ain't the way it should be done, but it could be." He went over it again. "He ain't got the right initials, but that's the order: section, township, range, and meridian. Ain't got the quarters, though. He ought to have the quarters."

"Can I see the records for that section?"

"If you want to, sure. That's what I'm here for."

He watched the old man finger his way down a row of tall, green-bound volumes, whose numbered patches were yellowing and curling away from the books' spines.

"Here. You can use that table. But if you take half the day like Orrin, I'm gonna charge you rent for it!"

"Yessir." He thumped the tome onto the table and folded back page after page until he came to the numerical heading he looked for. Whispering his finger down the column, he came to the right section. Wager carefully compared the cryptic numbers with the neatly lettered description in the book. Most of the page below was blank, and Wager supposed that was in case the quarters were divided into tracts. Only two of the quarters listed a recent change, and a notice of transfer of title named the new owner of both: Carmen Louisa Gallegos. It was dated four weeks ago. The taxable amount paid was $24,974.00. The previous owner, name carefully lined out but still legible, was Frederick Mueller.

Wager stared for a long time at the entry, trying to fit this new fact into Mueller's killing and the avenging angels. But these facts had too many sharp corners, and he couldn't slide them into any neat pattern.

"You find what you want? Don't want to have to charge you rent—hee!"

He had found something. But whether it was what he wanted or not was another question. "Do you record these land transfers?"

"No. County clerk does that. I'm the librarian. Don't put a mark in those books, and see to it that nobody else does, either."

"Does the buyer come in and show proof of purchase to record the sale?"

"What for? Lawyers do all that—title transfer, deed, what-all—nope, all I ever see are the books. Clerk gets a list of transfers and each week or two down he comes and copies them into the records." The yellow nose sniffed. "Prissy young fella—thinks he knows it all."

"Can you tell me where the clerk's office is?"

The old man could and did, telling Wager once more that he was seventy-seven going on seventy-eight, and just as healthy as when he was a young man of fifty. When Wager finally closed the door on the man's still-quacking voice, he sighed with relief and climbed out of the coolness of the subbasement toward the ground floor. The clerk of records' office was just off the domed pavilion. But Wager found little help there.

"No, Detective Wager. The parties don't have to come in to record a sale. All I need to see is a notarized bill stating legal description and the tender for tax purposes. If folks are smart they'll go through a lawyer and a title search, but a lot of people don't want to pay those fees. And they don't really need to if it's a simple transaction."

"Doesn't the transfer have to be signed in front of a notary?"

"Yes. The seller has to have his own notarized deed and positive proof of identification—driver's license with photograph, in most cases."

"What about the buyer?"

"What for? The seller's satisfied and proves it with his signature, and the buyer gets what he wants—the deed. Now if it's a trade of property, or a contract payment, or restricted sale—mineral rights, water rights—then the buyer has to be notarized, too, to show that he read the contract he signed. But a fee-simple, cash sale, he just gets title to the property. That's his proof of purchase."

"What happens to the notarized sale?"

"You mean after we record it downstairs? We mail it back to the buyer. It's his legal deed."

"You don't make a copy?"

"No. Not yet, anyway. We just enter it in the transaction book. It's an old-fashioned way of doing things, but we don't have the money for copiers and computers."

Wager repeated, just to be sure. "So the only notarized copy goes to the buyer after it's been recorded downstairs?"

"He's the only one who needs it."

Which meant that neither Wager nor anyone else could locate the notary who witnessed the seller's signature. "Do you have a lot of sales? Any big properties?"

"In the last few years, yes. We're getting a lot of vacation-home development, especially up in the mountains. But the biggest transfers are ranch land. A whole section's not uncommon on the desert side of the county."

"You don't remember the names of the people who buy? Or the notary?"

"Not usually. We check the notary's registration number to make sure it's current. Who are you talking about?"

"Carmen Louisa Gallegos. I wondered if you knew her."

"Gallegos? There must be a hundred Gallegoses in the

county. All related. You know how the Catholics feel about
birth control."

"I know."

In the Jeep, Wager sat and mulled over the information,
trying to determine what it was he'd found out. This was
what Orrin was excited about—he was sure of that.
Mueller dead on or about the time he sold his land to one
Carmen Gallegos. Robbery? Paid in cash and somebody
knew about it? Avenging angels robbing him? Why leave
a drawing? And why hasn't Gallegos come forward to
claim the land? Well, if Wager didn't have a clear idea of
where he was going he at least knew where he was—at a
point where he needed help. Cranking the Jeep's loud
starter, he turned toward the sheriff's office.

The older woman who operated the switchboard and
radios caught his eye when he came in. "Detective Wager!
You have an urgent call from Denver. There's a note on
your desk."

It said he was to call Chief Doyle immediately, and
beneath it were the three times that the same message
had been received.

"Can I use your phone?"

"Sheriff Tice said you could use his. He's in his office and
you can go right on in."

Wager did, Tice looking up from the day's stack of warrants to be served. "I'm going to have to give you a beeper,
Detective Wager. That phone's been jumping all morning
for you."

"I was working on Orrin's notebooks."

"Oh? Find out anything?"

"I'm not sure. . . . How long does it take for the county
to process an estate for someone who died without a will?"

"Intestate? Who?"

"Mueller. Mueller didn't leave a will, did he?"

Tice leaned against his swivel chair, eyes narrowing. "No, come to think of it, he didn't. Not that we found, anyway. But that's the DA's worry now."

"So how long would the DA take?"

"Oh, hell, there's no rush on it. Not for somebody like Mueller. Six or eight months. Now if there was a lot of property to liquidate or problems with titles, it might take a couple years."

"Do you know a Carmen Louisa Gallegos?"

"I know three Carmen Louisa Gallegoses in this county. God only knows how many more's around. Why?"

"A Carmen Louisa Gallegos bought Mueller's land just about the time he was killed. She paid almost twenty-five thousand dollars."

Tice's wrinkled lids half covered his eyes as if he were a lizard baking in the sun. "Now that's interesting."

"No money was found at Mueller's? No check or bankbook?"

The sheriff shook his head. "No receipt for sale either. But we weren't really looking for anything like that. We figured it was still his land."

"You inventoried the cabin?"

"Roy did. Took him two full days with all the junk Mueller'd stuck in there. But that's what Roy said it was, junk. No twenty-five thousand dollars, that's for sure." Tice chewed his lip. "There could be a hiding place—man like Mueller probably hid anything important. He was gone from that cabin weeks on end when he hired out."

"Maybe we should look again."

"Maybe we should." Tice nodded. "I think we should."

"Yates told me that Mueller's ranch was next to worthless."

"Got some timber on it. But most of that's second growth."

"Then why would anybody want to buy it?"

Tice shrugged. "Put a summer cabin on it, maybe; we're getting a little of that up there now."

"A whole quarter-section for a cabin?"

"If you like privacy, I guess. But it ain't worth no twenty-five thousand—you could buy Mueller's place and a dozen more for that much. Most of that land's straight up and down, Wager. You can't do much else but look at it. Sure as hell can't run cows on it." He added, "And nobody wants to pay to look at it either. That's what a lot of people up there are finding out."

"What do you mean?"

"Some people up there think the avenging angels will be after them next. They're trying to sell out. But nobody's buying because the land's only good for starving on."

"Because of Mueller?"

"That, and one damn fool claims he got a phone call from an avenging angel. But I think it was somebody just trying to scare him and that's what I told him. I couldn't do a damn thing about it anyway. But some people are scared up there."

"How long ago, Sheriff? Why wasn't that information passed on to Chief Doyle?"

Tice set his ball-point pen down and leaned forward. "I ain't obliged to pass a damn thing on to you or Doyle or anybody else, Wager. It was two, three days after Mueller was found, and you'd gone back to Denver, and Doyle didn't have his statewide commission set up. And as far as I know, there haven't been any more phone calls since."

"This person hasn't been able to sell his land?"

"Not that I know of. Who in hell would buy it?"

"Who bought Mueller's land?"

The wrinkled eyelids blinked slowly, Tice's flare of anger having gone to the one thing that attracted any good cop's mind: a puzzling fact. He picked up the telephone and pushed the Intercom button. A second later one of the clerks answered. "Esther, I want you to go over to the courthouse for me. I want you to look up any land sales in the last two weeks—northern half of the county. Let me know who's buying. Right away—thanks." He set the receiver on its cradle. "We can ask Roy, too. Here—make your call before Doyle claims I'm holding you incommunicado or something."

Wager dialed the familiar number and heard Doyle's secretary's voice answer with relief. "Yes, Detective Wager, one moment please."

"Wager? How are you? How's the eye?"

"No permanent damage the doc says."

"Fine. Glad to hear that. Any leads to who did it?"

"Nothing solid. Just a damn good guess."

"Uh-huh. On that," Doyle's voice pulled away from the telephone and then came back. "The FBI's forwarded some information from Mexican sources. Willis Beauchamp's religious group seems to have sent some men north. They've been under surveillance at the request of the local office since you came up with this polygamy thing. The report is that maybe fifteen men and boys loaded up and headed north. The FBI thinks they're in the States by now. Probably crossed illegally somewhere east of Douglas."

"How many?"

"Fifteen or so. They broke up into smaller groups for the crossing. Wager, the Mexican source says they came north well armed. He thinks they were coming up for some kind of religious war."

"How long ago?"

"Yesterday morning. The report came into FBI-Denver last night."

"They were still in Mexico when Orrin was shot?"

"Yes. But they probably intend to meet an advance party—which might be the ones who've been doing all the angel killings."

If they'd located the Kruses, and those survivors were by themselves, they wouldn't need that many people for a few women and kids. But if the surviving Kruses had found some friends . . . "So they're coming to finish it off."

"It looks that way."

Yesterday morning. They'd have to cross at night—last night. Then, if they pushed, they could reach Grant County sometime late today. Certainly by tonight.

"Wager, what kind of protection has that sheriff set up for those people out in the desert—the Winstons?"

"They didn't want any. They're hiding out. I'm sure the Kruse survivors are with them. But they claim they can take care of themselves."

"That's a bunch of crap."

Wager wasn't all that certain. "It's a hell of a gamble, anyway. I'll talk to the sheriff and see what he says."

"Right. If he needs anything he's to give me a call. The governor said we can use the National Guard if we need it. And one thing more—you're going to have reporters all over you like flies on stink. The wires picked up on that local story about the editor being killed—Orrin Winston— and they're sending people down. You might warn Tice."

"Will do." Wager hung up and Tice looked at him expectantly. "About fifteen armed men have come north from Mexico. Mexican sources say Willis wants to start a religious war. My guess is they're after Zenas Winston."

"Jesus Christ."

Or Yahweh or Mohammed or Joe Smith. Wager couldn't

remember if the Greeks ever fought a religious war; he thought they only fought over women or wealth. "It's still just a guess."

"I don't know of anybody else that Willis Beauchamp wants to get rid of."

"So what do we do?"

Tice's chair groaned with his reclining weight. "Tell you the truth, Wager, I'm not all that sure what there is to do."

It wasn't Wager's jurisdiction, but he had more than a passing interest in the case. "I've got an idea. But we'll have to move fast. And quiet."

"Let's hear it."

Wager told him.

10.

The first reporter called before noon, while Tice was still moving toward a grudging consideration of Wager's idea.

"If you've got a better plan," Wager said again, "let's hear it."

"Well, I don't. Not yet, anyway." Tice prowled once more to the Silex coffeepot and splashed another cup half full. "But damn it, Wager, this don't seem right. It may be the way you do things in Denver, but this ain't Denver."

"You could wait until after it's over and then try to catch them. Otherwise, I don't see what choice we have."

"Oh, hell, Wager! You—"

The telephone interrupted Tice and he spoke loudly into the receiver: "Sheriff Tice!" Wager saw the man's wrinkled eyelids droop slightly as if guarding a poker hand; and despite his irritation Wager realized that Tice had been re-elected for the last twenty years or so, and had built up his department among the hot jealousies of county politics.

"No, sir," said Tice, "we don't have a statement right now. We're working on it. Yes, sir, I've called in help. The

Colorado Bureau of Investigation is assisting with its technical services, and the Denver Police Department sent out a special homicide detective to help in the investigation." A slight smile, like a twist at the corner of Tice's mouth. "You can talk to him if you want. Sure." He held the telephone out to Wager. "It's a *Denver Post* reporter. Somebody called Gargle."

"Crap." He took the receiver. "Hello, Gargan. We don't know much so we can't tell you much."

"Wager? Jesus H. Christ, is that really you, Wager?"

"Yes."

"Oh, boy—wouldn't you know!" He could almost see Gargan's head shake. "Wager, I don't like it either, but I've got to work with you and that hayseed sheriff, and you've got to work with me."

" 'Got to,' Gargan?"

"Got to. It was a newsman that was murdered, Wager, and that's a national event. They've already had a report of it on the *Today Show*, and I came down on the Channel Four helicopter. It was one of our people that got killed, Wager; that's a front-page story. Wire services, national television, news magazines. This time, Wager, you've got to talk to me." A smile came into his voice. "Doyle said so."

"We have no idea who killed the man, Gargan."

"What about the drawing of the angel with a sword? The one they found on the victim? That sounds like a tie-in with the Denver murders. And what about the guy in the northern part of the county—Mueller?" His voice dropped. "And what about you getting shot at, Scarface? Do you tie that to the angel killings, too?"

"Gargan—"

"Come on now. This is a big story. I've put a lot of time in on it, Wager, and I've got a right to it!"

Wager covered the mouthpiece. "He's asking about me getting shot at. It won't be long before he finds out about

Willis Beauchamp coming north. Then we won't have a
chance."

"How in hell—?" Tice took the telephone. "This is Sheriff Tice, Mr. Gargle. We got an investigation going on here
and we got no comment to make yet. No, I don't, and I
don't care what your 'confidential sources' tell you. No sir,
Mr. Doyle don't tell me what to do in my own county.
When we do find out something, we'll let you know." He
hung up while the receiver was still squawking. Immediately, it rang again and Tice said "Who? Television? Goddamn it, Earl, I don't know nothing about them!"

A knock on the door, and Cynthia, her worried eyes still
avoiding Wager, leaned in to whisper, "Sheriff, it's a reporter from the *New Mexican* down in Santa Fe. She says
she'd like to ask you a few questions. Line three."

"Shut the goddamn door! No, not you, Earl. Those people can take all the damn pictures they want. Yes, and
interview any civilian they can catch: it's a free damn
country, Earl. But if I catch any sheriff's employee shooting off his mouth to any reporter, they're going to be
looking for another job!" He hung up and stared at Wager
with slightly wild eyes. "Jesus God, it's like the circus come
to town!" Then he glanced at the clock. "The morning
flight from Denver. It got in a half hour ago, didn't it?"

Wager shrugged; it wasn't his town, and now Gargan
belonged to the sheriff. "You're going to have to hold a
news conference soon. They've linked Orrin to the angel
killings. You might want to give Chief Doyle a call before
you make a statement. That way you two can coordinate
your news releases."

"I might, and by God I might not!" He pressed the
intercom button and a moment later Cynthia came back,
trying not to look flustered. "You give Nelly Winston a call
without them goddamn reporters hearing you—tell her to
find someplace to get where they can't hunt her down or

she won't get a minute's peace. Then get me that man Doyle in Denver."

"Time's getting short for Zenas, Sheriff."

"I know that, Wager! But I damn well don't like what you're suggesting."

As Wager had pointed out, Tice could come up with nothing better. The two men now stood in the day room of the county jail, the only place safe from the clusters of reporters and photographers who dashed after each other like kids chasing a football. Tice's stocky figure seemed heavier behind the wide cartridge belt that glinted with the oily brass of rifle bullets. He studied, one at a time, the nine uniformed men standing in line before him. Wager, feeling baggy in the oversized tan shirt and brown trousers of the Grant County sheriff's department, stood at the end of the line.

"That's all the information I can give you right now," Tice said quietly. "Now I'm not ordering you reserve officers to come with us. I'm asking you to, but any one of you that doesn't want to is free to leave, and no questions asked. Just keep your damn mouths shut about this here meeting."

"You ain't told us what it is you're asking us to do," said a nasal voice down the line.

"That's for security reasons. Anybody who stays will not be allowed to telephone or talk to anybody until after this operation's over—wife, sweetheart, nobody." He added grimly, "If it's what I think, it won't be no picnic. And not a damn one of us is getting paid enough to do what we might have to do." He waited a long moment, eyes moving up and down the line of faces. "All right—last chance.

This is going to be damn dangerous, and any of you reserve officers who want out, you're free to go right now."

From one of the newer and more carefully tailored uniforms near the middle of the line, a drawling voice said, "Hell, D.L., we don't get paid anyway. We might as well not get paid for this as not get paid for something else."

A couple of other voices chuckled, and all stood without moving.

"All right, boys, I appreciate it. And I know Earl and Roy do, too." He cleared his throat. "Now here's what we're going to do, and I don't want anybody outside this room to learn about it. Those destroying angels seem to get information quicker than the housewife's grapevine; and if they get wind of this, God only knows when we'll get another chance at them." Quietly, he told them the plan, not mentioning that it was Wager's idea initially, but taking all the responsibility for it on himself. When he finished, somebody gave a low whistle and asked, "Fifteen or more? Well armed?"

"We hope they won't be expecting to run across us. And we'll get some help from the Winstons." He added dryly, "We could call out the National Guard, I suppose, if we wanted the whole damn state to know about it."

From the other end of the line where he stood with Deputy Hodges, Yates asked, "Does Zenas Winston know we want to use him for bait?"

Tice winced. "I don't like to think of it that way, Roy. But if you or anybody else can come up with a better idea, let's hear it." He paused, but there was no answer. "All right, let's get the details worked out, because we don't have much time. This here's Detective Wager from the Denver Police." He pointed to the end of the line. "He'll be the second in command. Earl, you'll be in charge of Team One; Roy, you've got Team Two. Appoint yourselves a second in command just in case. I want you to draw radios and ammunition, and then move your teams out of here real quiet and in different directions so we got none of these newspaper people on our trails. You all know where we'll be going—the benchland—so you know what tack you'll need from your lockers. We'll rendezvous at Six Mile Spring at," he checked his watch, "three o'clock. That gives us time to get the horses there. One more thing," he said, "I want nobody bringing any whiskey. Not even a beer. Just water and plenty of it."

"No whiskey?" said a voice from the middle. "Damn, this must be serious!"

"It is. Let's head out now."

The men scattered quietly, with a curious glance or two in Wager's direction, but mostly with preoccupied looks pinching their eyebrows together. They followed their team leaders, Hodges or Yates, to the jail's armory to draw ammunition, and then to the shift room for their gear. Wager went with Tice back to the sheriff's office. There was something he wanted to check out before they left. Two pieces of the puzzle had clicked, almost unbidden, in the back of Wager's mind as he stood listening to Tice and watching the man's nervous, worried eyes. If it was what he thought, then some sense was beginning to emerge from the conflicting facts in the case. But with that sense came a feeling of foreboding as boundless and implacable as the desert they were about to enter.

"They're a good bunch of boys." Tice sighed as he settled into the creaking chair behind his desk. "I pray to God nothing happens to a single one of them."

"It's the only way," Wager said absently; his mind was

still on the department's radio logs that Esther, the woman at the radio console, had let him study.

"I know that. Or I sure as hell wouldn't be doing it."

"Do you want to call Doyle and tell him about it?"

Tice shook his head. "It's my responsibility, Wager. Not yours, not his. Mine. Besides, if that Denver reporter knew about you getting shot, then I think you got some security problems right in your own backyard, boy." He ran a finger down a list of telephone numbers taped to the glass on his desk. It was for a corral that rented riding horses and pack mules to local dude ranches and outfitters. "Mary Jo? This here's Daryl Tice. I'm going to need some horses and tack delivered out to Six Mile Spring. It's an emergency, but I don't want any noise about it, all right?"

Six Mile Spring was at the end of a road different from the one Wager had taken with Orrin. A small pool of water seeped from somewhere beneath a tangle of wind-sculpted boulders and ran in a short stream over the black roots of thick willows before sinking just as mysteriously into the grit. Two by two, the horses were led to the shallow water, where they bent and sucked loudly, their hind legs stamping to jar off the flies. Tice explained that a horse trail shortened the distance to Zenas's ranch by several miles, and that the party could twist down the shelves of rock and sand without raising dust like a column of automobiles would. "You and me," he added, "we'll drive over. One Jeep with two people in it won't scare off Willis. In fact, if he's anywhere around he might suspect something if he didn't see some kind of official activity."

Wager looked at the rangy horses being blanketed and saddled, their tails switching nervously, and nodded with relief. He'd ridden a horse years ago when he was a kid, and the only thing he remembered about it was the raw chafe of rear end and thighs that had been the result of an hour's ill-governed jolt around a level and well-marked horse trail.

When the last of the saddles had been unloaded from the pickup trucks that hauled the four-horse trailers, and the corral's drivers had pulled away in a clank of couplings and chains, Tice called the deputies together for a final briefing.

"You boys know the trail and you know time's short. Stake your horses down by Jones Bend—there's enough feed and water there, and you're only a mile or so from Zenas's place. Move up on foot and keep it quiet. No radio talk. When you're in sight of the ranch, give me three clicks on your transmitter, Earl. Three clicks, wait three seconds, then three more clicks, got that? We ain't going to take the chance they got a scanner somewhere."

Hodges nodded and spit.

"You move up low and quiet and get under cover," Tice repeated. "Then give me the clicks and I'll come out and find you—I know which way you'll be coming from."

"You figure on getting there before we do?" asked Yates.

"I sure don't aim to waste time on the road. But if we're late just sit tight and wait. You'll see us coming through the notch Be sure you stay out of sight at all times."

"Right."

Wager and Tice watched the column of horsemen quickly disappear among the interlaced willows, the occasional knock of a hurried hoof loud in the silence. The pungent smell of fresh horse droppings hung briefly in the air until a gust of hot wind blew it away. Then, wordless, Tice put the Jeep in gear and pulled out rapidly.

Their road, scarcely marked in the sand between widely

spaced clumps of seemingly dead brush, led south along the edge of one of the stony benches. Ahead, in the rising afternoon wind, a dust devil swirled, erect in a wavering column. It thickened to a solid core of whirling sand that whipped rapidly up the slope, then lifted to disappear as a faint tan smudge against the heat-paled sky. Now and then a gully notched the stone rim and gave Wager a glimpse of tumbled and shattered rock falling away like bleached bones toward the next bench of earth five hundred, a thousand feet below. In the distance beyond that he made out the channeled blue that marked the sky over the river. But the countless spurs and thrusts of contorted mesa walls gave him no idea at all of the site of Zenas's ranch.

"Is there any other way Willis can get to the ranch?"

"If you know the desert, sure. Six Mile Spring trail's one. But I don't think they'll use that, not if they're coming up from Mexico." Tice lifted his mirrored sunglasses and wiped his forehead with his arm, then resettled them. "Most likely, they'll come up from the southwest—there's roads enough across the Navaho reservation if you know where you're going. And they do. Willis was born and raised out there."

"How close can they drive?"

"Ten, maybe twelve miles. Then they got to walk. The Frying Pan Trail follows along the river, so they'd have plenty of water."

Wager tried to picture the column of armed men stumbling across the red and sun-heated rock down below the twisting lip of river gorge. "Can they be spotted from the air?"

"Sure. If they stand out in the open and jump up and down."

He let the sarcasm go. "When they run—if they run—we might call in an air search to round them up. Doyle can get the National Guard helicopters for us."

Tice shook his head. "Not even a helicopter can get in some of those cracks. An air search is all right if you're looking for somebody who wants to be found. But there's too many places where a man can curl up and hide. No." He shook his head once more. "It's got to be on the ground, and I hope to hell we're lucky."

They bounced in silence, Tice picking his way as quickly as he could along the crumbling rim. The scattered clumps of desert brush gave way to a valley so wide that Wager would not have noticed it if the Jeep's motor had not slackened. Juniper trees no taller than a man stood far apart, dotting the slope like sentinels, and at the valley's bottom spread a delta of rippled sand. When the Jeep's motor once more strained uphill, Tice bobbed his head. "The road's just up on that ridge. Then we can make some good time."

With the last few dragging, jouncing miles, Wager's mind had returned to an earlier question, one there hadn't been time to ponder in Tice's busy office. "Is there any way Orrin or Mueller could have learned about Willis's plans?"

Tice steered around a broken outcropping of pitted sandstone. "You mean that's why they might have been killed?"

"Just another possibility."

The sheriff chewed it over. "Maybe Orrin found out something. Damned if I can see how, though. Mueller, no. Too long ago. It would be before the Kruses ever got to Zenas's ranch. If they got there."

That was true. And it didn't tie into the sale of Mueller's land to this Carmen Louisa Gallegos. "Did your clerk Esther ever find out anything at the courthouse?"

The sheriff grunted. "I forgot to ask. All this news of Willis, and the goddamn reporters . . ." He keyed his microphone, calling his code number to the dispatcher. Only static answered. "Can't get there from here, I guess. Maybe up on the ridge."

They finally lurched up the last bit of slope and turned onto the now-familiar dirt road. Tice tried the radio again, getting a faint, thin voice in return, "Go ahead, go ahead. I'm receiving you."

"What did Esther find out at the courthouse? I'm in a hurry."

"Wait one."

They fidgeted in the hot wind that blew through the open sides of the Jeep and carried a fine grit that clogged the nose and crackled faintly between the teeth.

"She says no sales recorded . . ." Static broke the transmission. ". . . has been trying to buy options."

"Say again—you're breaking up."

"She says no sales recorded last two weeks. But her uncle told her that somebody's been trying to get options on all the land that's up for sale."

"Ten-four. Any name on that somebody?"

Static. Tice tried again and then said, "To hell with it, the band's breaking up. Options wouldn't be recorded anyway. Let's move—we've wasted enough time." He plunged the Jeep in gear and tore through the sand toward the next series of switchbacks.

They paused at the notch that overlooked the Winston ranch. The line of Lombardy poplars tracing the main irrigation ditch cast shadows like a giant picket fence across the shaggy surface of the cornfield. The square house sat in the deep shade of the cottonwoods, and behind it the sun on the river glinted a quivering silver. Out of the trees came the startled squawk of a blue jay, and then only the wind.

Tice used his binoculars to scan the surrounding rock walls, quartering the vista and working methodically and slowly through each section. Finally he said, "Nothing. Not even a dog. They've pulled out." He dropped the roughly idling Jeep into low gear for the sharp descent.

"We're ahead of Willis?"

"I didn't see any buzzards." Tice added, with that twist at the corner of his mouth, "But if he did beat us, I hope he's had time to leave before you and me get there."

Dust swirling around them, they pulled to a stop in front of the house. Tice killed the motor and they sat in the Jeep, the radio giving a muted hiss, waiting. The sheriff was right about the dogs; no frantic barking, no nervous bleats from the penned goats broke the silence. Only the soft chatter of cottonwood leaves blending with the rush of the shallow river.

"How long does it take from Six Mile Spring to where they leave the horses?"

"Couple hours. But it's a long country mile from Jones Bend, and the boys can't walk too damn fast in cowboy boots. A lot of it's across slickrock, too."

It took another half hour; the blue jay jabbered occasionally, and once they heard the distant, rusty croak of a crow gliding the updrafts above the cliffs. But no voices came from the house or the trees surrounding it.

Zenas could see them, Wager knew. But the man was not going to show himself in the open. He would wait, like last time, until they were close enough to be called quietly into the shelter of the bushes. And that would take as long as Hodges and Yates needed to sneak into hiding nearby.

Tice's thick fingers drummed restlessly on the steering wheel. Gradually, the shadow of the stone house moved toward the Jeep's square bumper, touched the dusty knobbed tire, rose an inch or so up its bulging, dusty flank.

When the signal came, it was sharp and strong, three

clicks like river stones popped together, a short silence, then three more clicks. Tice thumbed his receiver twice in reply and then heaved out of the driver's seat. "Let's find Zenas."

The two men stood briefly, eyes searching the cliffs, ears listening through the liquid sound of the cottonwoods. Out of courtesy, they knocked at the door of the house they knew to be empty. Then Wager led Tice around the side toward the barn. "He was waiting in those willows last time."

He was again, his soft voice greeting them when they were halfway across the barnyard. "If you come in peace come this way."

"I don't know how much peace we bring," said Tice. "But we got to talk."

They pushed through the tangled screen of willow branches. Zenas, rifle ready, kneeled to peer past the two until they were totally hidden. Then he gestured at them to sit down. "What is it this time?"

"It's nice to see you, too, Zenas." Tice crouched heavily on one knee and panted against the bind of his cartridge belt. "We got word this morning that Beauchamp's come north with about fifteen armed men. We figure they're looking for you and the Kruses."

Zenas's hand stroked lightly down his beard. "Fifteen. That's a lot. He comes looking for blood atonement then."

Wager raised his eyebrows.

Tice explained, "That's where you wash away a man's sins with his own blood. It's a lot more convenient than using your own."

Zenas's dark eyes widened slightly with anger. "You may mock, Tice, but a man's flesh is only temporal. His soul is eternal. Eternal!"

The sheriff grunted. "Let the good Lord look after the souls. My job's to look after the flesh. And that's what I'm here to do, Zenas, like it or not. I want to get me some destroying angels."

"They are not Danites—they don't labor with the blessing of the Lord. They are apostate!"

"They sure don't labor with the blessing of the law. That's why we're here."

"With the help of the Lord, we will look after our own. We don't need you."

"You need every gun you can get and you know it."

The bearded man could not bring himself to agree, but his silence marked the truth of what Tice said.

"Counting me and Detective Wager, we got ten rifles. Eight of them are already in place."

"I know," said Zenas, a glint of cold humor in his eyes. "My son watched them come in from Jones Bend. You gave him a good scare."

Tice poked at the soft dirt with a twig. "I figured you got all the trails watched. You've seen nothing of Willis then?"

Zenas shook his head.

"He's coming. Maybe tonight. Maybe tomorrow or the next day. But he's coming. You believe me, don't you?"

"Even so."

"I'd like to set a trap for him."

Interest rippled behind the blank expression Zenas wore for Gentiles.

"I'd like you to put your family back in the house so we can draw them in. Then we can get them before they scatter."

"No."

Tice poked again. "If we get them they'll be out of your hair. If we don't they'll be back. How long you think they'll take to find where you've got your people hid?"

"I'll not sacrifice one of my family."

"Nobody's talking sacrifice, Zenas. We'll have people inside the house and outside. And when Willis comes in we'll close on him fast. He won't be expecting as many guns as he'll find."

"He will plan for the worst and hope for the best, and he has all the guile and craft of the Antichrist. If you fail then he has my family. I will not bring them into that danger."

"Well, I can't deny there'll be some danger." Tice scratched his ear. "God alone knows what can go wrong. But if it works and we do get him we can put him away for a long time. Him and all the people with him."

"My family is a sacred trust. It is our duty to God to work his will on earth. No one else—Gentile, infidel, Antichrist—no one else has been chosen for this duty and this joy." The words came out like pebbles tossed on the ground between them. "If I bring harm on those who are God's true laborers then my soul will wander unregenerate and so will theirs. What you want, Tice, is that I risk not only their lives but their eternal bliss in the highest heaven. I won't do it."

Wager spoke for the first time, trying to keep exasperation from his voice. "Maybe it's God's will we're here," he said. "I don't know. I don't think you do either. But we both know what that man wants to do, and it won't be just your family that's in danger; it'll be the rest of the people in your church, too. If Beauchamp's not caught, none of you are safe. Look." Wager pointed through the thick tangle at the house. "He outnumbers us. But if we can pen them in a small area and catch them by surprise we've got a chance, and a good one. The way to do that is to make the ranch seem normal so they will move in close. God, or somebody, has given you this chance to get Willis. You ask your people —see if some of them are willing to take the risk. If they are it won't all be on your soul if something happens."

Zenas's eyes narrowed with thought. "Despise not wisdom though it be from the serpent himself."

Wager wasn't sure if he liked that serpent bit, but he saw that the man was weighing the argument. He and Tice waited; the only sounds were the rustling leaves and the occasional *zing* of a hurrying insect.

"I will ask my sons."

"It's got to look real," said Wager again. "It's got to look natural enough to fool Beauchamp into coming in close."

Zenas added grudgingly, "And my women. But you two will have to be in there, too."

It was nearing sunset by the time Tice had briefed his men, warning them repeatedly against smoking and unnecessary talk or movement. "We want as many of them in as possible before we make our move. We don't want to scare them off. If it works you hold your fire until I call you in—everybody got that?"

Silent nods from the men seated or sprawled on the cooling sand of the small, deep crevice that served as an assembly area.

"Don't move up to your positions until just at dark. And then, by God, you set still and keep quiet. If it don't happen tonight pull back to this assembly area as soon as you can see your fingers in front of your face."

"How long you think this'll take, Sheriff?" asked the nasal voice.

Tice shrugged. "It can't be too long—Willis won't want to stay in the States too long. Two, three days at most, I'd say. Why, you in a hurry to get someplace?"

"He's in a hurry to get his pecker dipped before somebody else gets there."

"You be go to hell," said Nasal. "If you could even get yours up you'd maybe know something about it!"

"That's enough," said Tice. "Now I don't want any horseplay from you people. This here's damn serious, and we got a lot of lives we're responsible for—women and children. You hear me?"

The nasal voice mumbled a "Well, he started it. . . ."

"Now, Wager and me are going to drive out like we're leaving. When it gets dark, we'll double back and set up in the house. Remember, if they come tonight don't anybody spook them—let them take the bait good, you hear me? We'll raise enough hell so they think they got the whole bunch trapped and bring up everybody. Then— and only then—you people make your move. I'll radio for you." Tice paused to give emphasis: "We only have one chance. I don't want nobody screwing it up. Earl, you and Roy got any questions? Anybody else?"

There were none. Tice and Wager shared cold camp with the group and then picked their roundabout way back through a series of cracks and fissures between the cooling and gigantic rocks toward the farmhouse. As they approached the shelter of the trees, they heard wood being chopped and the loud rattle of cooking pans carried on the breeze.

"Well, I guess you talked him into it," said Tice. "You old serpent."

Zenas had brought only three of his family: his first wife, Miriam, and two boys between ten and twelve years old. Those two watched the approaching strangers with large, solemn eyes; their shotguns, almost as tall as they were, leaned handily inside the kitchen door. Miriam, her graying hair in a tight bun at the back of her neck, avoided glancing at either Gentile; but her worry trailed behind her like an odor as she strode through the kitchen and downstairs rooms, lighting the fire in the stove as the afternoon cooled into evening, carrying oil lamps from window to window, attending to all the business of getting a large farm family ready for supper. And sharply bossing the two boys, as if she did not think they should be there.

Zenas led them silently through the house and out the front door toward their Jeep. He stood casually in the softening light, a clear target for any sniper who might be working toward them from one of the surrounding cliffs. "When you come back, come up the back way past the outhouse. I'll have the dogs penned up, but don't try to come in until you get an answer to your signal."

"All right," said Tice. "Be about an hour, hour and a half."

"I'll be here," he said laconically, and without another word turned back to the house, whose windows glowed more brightly in the dusk that rose from the canyon floor.

"Did he tell you where his family's hidden?" Wager asked.

"No. But I can guess." Tice steered over a rough ledge of rock lifting like a spine across the dirt road. "There's three or four big canyons downriver a couple miles. My guess is he's got them scattered out there." He added, "That's probably Willis's guess, too, if this little trick don't fool him. I hope to God this trick works."

"Those two kids," said Wager, "they make it look real. But they sure are young."

"They can pull a trigger if they have to. Things work out, they won't have to."

Wager looked over his shoulder at the ranch below, a cluster of pale lights in the dark bank of trees. A plume of smoke rose from the chimney against the clear green of the desert evening. The wind had hesitated again and the smoke stood like a ghostly flagpole against the sky. "Did he leave his oldest sons on guard there?"

"Yes. And I didn't try to talk him out of that. If they hear shooting up here most of them are supposed to move upriver and close off the west side. If the shooting starts down there we run like sonsofbitches and try to save whoever we can."

"How far away is it?"

"About a half hour if you walk."

A lot of people could be killed in a half hour. "How many guns does he have down there?"

"Six."

So if Willis didn't split his people he would outnumber either group of defenders. "It's got to work," said Wager.

"Yep," said Tice.

Gradually, the headlights became stronger, picking out boulders tumbled at the roadside and then gliding past them to fall away into the dark above the sandy track. The main road swung into the headlights, leading uphill as the Jeep ground and lurched through the sand. To the south a faint orange glow stuttered a moment, then turned black again as a thunderstorm built up over the mountains a hundred miles distant. A minute or two later another flicker, silent as distant artillery, answered from a different corner of the horizon.

"Late moon tonight. Won't be up before twelve, one o'clock."

In Vietnam, when the patrols had rotated around to his platoon, Sergeant Wager had felt this same sense of suspension, as if he were cut off from both past and future. That's how it had been when everything was ready and there was nothing to do except wait: a feeling like the one he had now—separate, tightly held, curiously relaxed.

"I reckon this is far enough." Tice flipped off the lights and drove a hundred or so more yards down the gray track before turning from the road. "We can hide the Jeep in this ravine. It'll be pretty much out of sight come light."

"Fine."

The desert air, cooling quickly, was especially sharp

after the searing heat of the day. Wager pulled on the dark brown uniform jacket he had been loaned and snapped the cuffs. Without wasting words, the two men took their rifles out of the Jeep and began to trudge back down the road into the black reaches of the canyon.

11.

They heard the music before the farmhouse lights winked through the notch. Following the calm of the long, green twilight, the awakened breeze's restless shiftings carried the thin wail of a fiddle first from one corner of the rocky canyon, then from another.

"That noise doesn't soothe any savage beast I know of," murmured Wager.

Tice grunted. "Mormons like their music. Zenas is probably doing what they do every night—having some music, praying, and then going to bed."

"Beats watching television."

"It does that. Especially if you don't have electricity."

Tice led away from the road and along a trail of dirt that glimmered between dark sandstone blocks tumbled from the cliffs above. They gradually worked their way into the shelter of the black trees bordering the river and then toward the rear of the farmhouse. By the time they drew near, the music had stopped. One by one, the glowing windows darkened until only the back of the house showed any lights. Pausing a stone's throw away, the sheriff folded his hands into a hollow fist and blew softly on his bent thumbs; the furry whistle, like the call of an owl, echoed through the rustling leaves around them.

He blew a second time.

The kitchen lights went out; a single window upstairs gleamed yellow behind breeze-ruffled curtains.

Wager heard it first, a faint hissing between clamped teeth, then he saw the stubby shadow dart and pause and dart again from the bulky shape of the house.

"Over here," he whispered.

The boy, panting lightly with excitement, sprinted to them. "Pa says follow me. Stay low."

They moved cautiously in a zigzag pattern from shadow to bush, finally gliding along the rough stone walls to a dim corner where a window stood open.

"Pa says come in this way," the boy whispered, and slithered quickly up to the flat sill.

Wager followed, the stones warm beneath his gripping fingers. Tice handed him the rifles, and, stifling a heavy grunt, hauled himself over the ledge with a relieved sigh, then rested a moment in the dark room to catch his breath. "Where's your pa?" he asked softly.

"He's upstairs. Seeing to Aunt Miriam."

"Seeing to her?"

The boy's grin could be sensed in the dark. "It's her turn," he whispered. "She told him she was the first and if the Lord willed that she be the last, it was up to Pa to abide the Lord's will."

Tice muttered something indecipherable.

"Where's your brother?" asked Wager.

"Taking stuff out to the root cellar. Pictures and stuff. You really think the Antichrist is coming tonight?"

"There's a good chance," Wager said.

"Gol'!"

After a while they heard a creak on the stair and Zenas's

hushed voice followed from somewhere in the black house. "Daniel? You, Daniel!"

"Here, Pa. I got them."

"All right. You let the dogs loose, and then you and Ezra go upstairs. You remember where you're supposed to stay?"

"Yes, Pa."

"Good, son. The Lord's blessing and mine are with you both."

"Thank you, Pa." The short shadow scurried excitedly through the dark room to the corner window and in a blink dropped out of sight. A moment later the men heard the thumping patter of animal feet and a happy snuffling in the outside night.

"There's apple juice and bread set out if you want it."

"I am thirsty," Tice told him. "I reckon you ought to be, too."

Zenas did not answer, and they settled down to wait in the dark, silent house.

As the sheriff had said, the moon came up between midnight and one. It wasn't Wager's watch, but he lay awake on a blanket folded on the bare floor of the dining room and looked at the pale light grow stronger through the restless trees to the west. After uncountable minutes the moon cleared the eastern lip of the canyon and reflected brightly off the rock walls behind the trees. But the canyon shadow still sheltered the house and the grove, and the glow made the darkness covering them seem even thicker.

In the quiet of the rooms, the sense of suspension returned to Wager. Reaching a finger under the pad of gauze, he gently pressed the wounded eye to feel for soreness. There was an answering pulse to the weight of his finger, a reminder of the flesh. It brought Wager back to the puzzling question of the differences between the angel deaths in Denver and those in Loma Vista. But despite the different circumstances or causes, the same angel appeared. An exact copy of the angel of death. Of vengeance. Of righteous murder. Yet why Mueller and his worthless land that Carmen Gallegos had paid so much for?

Sleepless, he lay and turned the different parts over in his mind. Mueller's ranch, and that Carmen Louisa Gallegos that nobody could find. Kruse's family disappearing, and probably here at Zenas's farm. The break-in at Orrin's office. The slaughtered Beauchamps. It had to make sense. Somehow it had to make sense.

Sometime after two, when he had slid into that floating area between sleep and waking, Wager heard a board creak beneath his head, and an instant later a hand pressed his shoulder.

"I'm awake," he whispered.

Tice's lurching breath whispered back. "Zenas heard something around the outbuildings. He says the goats are getting upset about something."

Wager rolled to his feet and went quickly to the window in the kitchen. Beyond the rusty screen the windy night was filled with the sounds of motion: the rattle and hiss of leaves, the toss of the shallow river over its rocky bed, the hum of insects. But that was all he heard. The moonlight had dimmed and had dropped lower down the far wall, and he strained his good eye for any movement against its glow. "Is he out there?" Wager murmured.

"No. He's over by the front door."

Through the dry rustle of the leaves he heard the leaden *clank* of an animal's bell. The dogs were still silent; Wager didn't see how anyone could creep up to the farmhouse without waking one of those dogs into hysterical yapping. Behind him he sensed more than heard Tice's figure glide away through the dark house to peer and listen at one of the other windows. Then Wager thought he saw something. Blinking his eye, he pressed against the screen and shifted his gaze slightly from side to side to make the best use of his off-center vision. It was a little trick he'd learned along the DMZ and it had later saved his tail more than once in Vietnam. He hoped it worked with just one eye. Holding his breath, he peered intently at the humanlike shadows of trees and shrubs dim in the moonglow.

There.

Wager saw it this time.

A black, humped shadow sprinted half a dozen steps across a background of moonlit river, then silently blended with the frayed blackness of the bushes.

"Tice!" Wager eased back from the window and hissed the man's name as loudly as he dared. "Tice—they're coming in!"

No answer.

Wager groped through the unfamiliar room toward the parlor where Zenas was supposed to be. But before he reached it, he heard a scratching at the kitchen door, then a metallic click and the dry slide of the lock's metal tongue. Then he saw the pale square of the door slowly begin to swing open.

Stifling his breath, Wager eased the safety off his Star PD and knelt to brace his arm across his thigh. The door swung back steadily to show an empty square of moonglow. He leveled the pistol and waited. The sound came before he saw anything: the cautious slipping of a body across the low sill, the hesitant silence of an invisible hand probing ahead in the dark. Then he saw the darkness at the bottom of the doorway move, and the ill-formed shadow of a figure crawled in. The shape paused and listened, and Wager hoped that his kneeling outline, not ten feet from the peering man, blended into the other shadows like one more chair. The shape rose slowly beside the open door, and Wager could make out the outline of a head and shoulders. He heard a slight rustle and a moment later the tiny, sharp gleam of a pen-light winked twice toward the trees.

It took maybe five seconds. Through the wind came the muffled thud of heels, and a line of dark figures too blurred to count crossed the small patch of moonlight just beyond the kitchen. He let the first two or three enter, their panting breath stifled and movements clumsily cautious in the dark. Then he squeezed the trigger and dove for the doorway leading to the dining room.

The muzzle flash stripped the shadows from a half-dozen men crowding into the room and gleamed orange against their bulging eyes. Wager clearly saw the nearest one, a figure with a mud-smeared face and a chest-length gray beard. The figure started to swing a long-barreled revolver even as the shock of the pistol round jerked his mouth open into a startled gape. Then a shotgun exploded in the close room, its blast hot and deafening, and he felt the wind from a heavy lead plug whip across the back of his neck as he dove. Kicking the door shut and blinking frantically to clear the muzzle glare from his eyes, Wager rolled into a tangle of chairs as the shotgun's second barrel blasted through the wood panels to send splinters whining across the table over his head. He fired two quick rounds low at the door and rolled again, banging his head on the table leg to escape an answering volley that filled the length of the black room with the thudding crackle of slugs. Somewhere behind him he heard Tice's voice shout something, and a rifle, numbingly loud, boomed from the hallway toward the kitchen. Wager's rifle had been sent spinning from his side, but he had no time to grope for it now. The close muzzle blasts were like a furious wind that pressed him flat against the wooden floor behind the thin shelter of the overturned table.

"Outside!" Tice was shouting, "Outside!" And then Wager heard it, the clump of sprinting boots and the crash of breaking glass as men ran from the kitchen to circle around through the windows. One shadow bobbed just over Wager's head and he snapped a quick shot at it with his pistol. The blast and shattering glass almost covered the man's howl. A flicker of orange rifle fire lit the front parlor and Zenas's rifle boomed an answer. Wager emptied his clip into the splintered kitchen door, ripping it off its hinges as bullets from an automatic thundered past him, and he scuttled and rolled frantically toward the stairs. Trying to dodge among the flickering shadows, he fumbled for a new clip to jam into his pistol while he yanked himself around a door frame and lay gasping and suddenly cold in his own sweat.

Beside him a rifle fired-pumped-fired-pumped-fired as Tice, his bulk wedged into a corner of the hallway, covered Wager's desperate, sprinting crawl.

Then silence.

It felt like silence—his ears still roared and tingled, but the hot concussions of the automatic weapon did not punch against his flesh, and the sting of burning powder no longer seared his weeping eye.

"You okay Wager?" panted Tice. "Wager?"

"Yeah. You?"

"Gut shot."

Wager crawled to the shadow looming in the corner. "How bad?"

"Can't tell. I'm still numb."

Zenas's rifle suddenly fired again and, from outside, an answering barrage from several rifles splattered slugs against the groaning stones of the house. A shatter and a flash lit the parlor; Zenas yelled "Fire," and a voice in the dark howled, "That's him—the Judas-devil!—get him!" Then gunfire blasted over the voices.

"Call in the deputies!"

"Can't." Tice pushed the radio across the floor to Wager. "Broke—shot."

"Goddamn!" Running blindly, Wager took the stairs two at a time, calling out "Don't shoot—I'm the cop!" toward the two frightened boys he knew to be huddled somewhere in the blackness of the second floor, their shotguns aimed toward the sound of his shoes. Below, the firing had started again, this time with less frantic intensity. It settled into measured explosions designed to keep them pinned down until the flames did their work or the people coming in through the kitchen could hunt them down one by one. Smoke followed Wager, unseen but stinging in his nose, and he fumbled through the unfamiliar hall for a door that would lead to a window. His fingers brushed the panels and found a knob. He twisted and pushed, but it was locked. And no doubt one of the boys—or maybe the woman—crouched across the room with a gun, ready to blow away the first figure who broke through. He slid down the wall to the next door, finding it open and seeing the pale rectangle of window in the far side. Banging his shins against the crowded bedsteads, he fumbled to the window and stood aside to aim his pistol at the stars. He hoped to hell the deputies would guess what he meant. He squeezed off three measured rounds. The weak sound of his pistol made mild pops against the heavier rifle fire, and from the trees below came the red flash and scattered crackle of buckshot aimed up at his window. Wager groped his way back toward the stairs through the thickening smoke of the hallway, where now a dim and pulsing glow began to tint the walls.

"Ezra?" Wager hissed. "David . . . where in hell are you?"

"It's Daniel," answered a shaking whisper. "They're shooting down our whole house! It's awful—they're shooting down our whole house—where's Pa?"

"He's all right—he's okay. Where in hell's your brother?"

"Down here. He's crying. You shouldn't cuss. God won't like it." The voice trembled again. "God won't like it and we need Him!"

Praying wouldn't help either. "It'll be all right, Daniel. You're a big boy—you look after your brother. Tell him your pa's all right. Listen: Is there a way out of here? Can you get down some way?"

"Yessir." The voice steadied a bit. "Pa put a rope ladder in the big bedroom. In case of fire."

"Good. You get your brother and your mother and go in there. Stay there until you can't stay any longer, and then get out—fast. By that time the deputies ought to be here." Maybe. At least it was a chance. A better chance than the Beauchamp kids had against that blood-smeared toilet bowl.

"She's not our ma, she's our aunt."

"Just do it, damn it!"

"Yessir." The figure ran to the locked door and knocked softly.

Wager started down the dimly lit stairwell, blinking against the acrid smoke and feeling his way along the smooth wall, pistol flicking back and forth in front of him.

Zenas was still shooting. The boom of his weapon moved from spot to spot as he darted from window to window. The answering fire thumped solidly against the outside stones or screamed in fragments through the smoky darkness to tear softly into the plaster. From the sound, Wager could tell that they had spread out to surround the farmhouse and wait for the fire to burn them out. Then beneath the blasts he heard a new sound, a low, steady grunting that told him the shock had ebbed from Tice's wound and the pain was beginning.

"Tice?" Wager whispered to the slumping figure in the corner. "Tice! Hang on—they should be here soon."

"Yeah. Fire. Use rugs . . ."

Wager glanced through the dark dining room toward the shattered kitchen door, behind which he thought he heard murmurs. Lunging across the line of fire, he crawled into the parlor to find Zenas crouched between the exploded windows reloading his rifle with dully gleaming cartridges. Wager felt the short, thick nap of carpet and yanked at it as a bullet whacked just over his head and sent plaster chips and a hot, jagged scrap of copper across his back. The fire had burned blue and spread in an oily, flickering ring down one wall and out over the floor, where a draft fed one side. As he watched, the flames turned yellow with fresh life and began to dart higher. He threw the carpet wide, hitting with his hands at the hotness beneath. Zenas, drawing a deep breath as an eddy of fresh air swirled through the broken windows, gasped, "Did Tice call in the deputies?"

"Radio's shot." Wager dragged the smoking carpet over to another section of flame.

"Lord help us," muttered Zenas. "I figure it's been four, maybe five minutes. It'll take my boys a good fifteen to come up the canyon. Pretty soon Beauchamp'll guess there's only a few of us in here."

Only four or five minutes since the first, hurried shot. It seemed like years. "We can't last that long."

"I know that."

A sudden blast of slugs shocked the air around them and Zenas swung his rifle up to the glass-littered sill. "Here comes another torch," he called, and fired two quick shots before ducking to avoid the scream of answering bullets.

Wager heard Tice trying to yell something.

"What is it?"

"Kitchen—coming through the kitchen." His voice choked. "You and Zenas upstairs. Now!"

"Come on!" Behind him he heard Zenas scuttle through the glass. Tice fired into the kitchen to pin the invaders down as the two men stumbled up the stairs. Zenas leaped ahead, and halfway up Wager stopped to fire a round and call, "Now, Tice, come on up!"

"Go!" The bulky shape flung an arm at him and fired again. Then the automatic exploded in a solid wall of heat and concussion and hammering slugs that drove Wager up the stairs as the bannister disintegrated beneath his hand.

On the upper landing Zenas was calling into the smoke-filled darkness. "Ezra! Daniel!"

"They're in the big bedroom." Wager coughed. "The one with the rope ladder."

"My woman?"

"Her, too."

"Good." He pointed Wager to his right. "You go down there. I'll go here. We can put a crossfire at the top of the stairs."

Wager quickly felt his way to an open doorway as, below, Tice's rifle boomed again. The sheriff couldn't get out of his corner, but no one could get in either. Not without facing that rifle he used so well; not unless the fire worsened and smoked him out. Or they came in through the front. They were still firing steadily at the front, but soon they'd notice no return fire.

Wager, his skin fried and oily from the gunpowder and smoke, knocked apart a bed frame to pile up a low shelter that angled out into the hallway. If they got past Tice, if they came up those stairs, it would have to be one at a time. Wager and Zenas could hold them off if they tried that, unless Willis's men just sat back and let the house burn down. That's what Wager would do in the attackers' place—let it burn and pick them off one at a time as they fled.

Outside the rifle fire increased and Wager heard it build to cover a rush toward the front door. The automatic in the kitchen let loose, too, quivering even the masonry walls with its deep, punching blasts. But it sounded different, as though it was turned away from the house. Then Wager realized that the growing rifle fire formed a ring of constant explosions that was closing in on the house quickly and savagely. The deputies—Zenas's people, somebody—had come, and their gunfire was washing over the attackers from behind, scattering them, shifting their fire, driving them toward the shelter of the smoking, splintered farm-house that would become their trap, too. Wager ran to the window and saw the circumference of gun flashes move quickly among the trees. Here and there it tangled in close and desperate glare, but steadily it pressed toward the house. Then he heard the front door kicked open and the clatter of boots and an urgent, frightened voice calling orders. A second later the house trembled from the roar of rifles and the stomp of running boots, and through the din Wager heard vague shouts and the sound of heavy feet leaping up the stairs. He steadied his pistol and when the first figure appeared on the landing, red and gigantic in the light from the flames below, he fired. The figure howled shrilly and fell back out of sight, to be immediately re-placed by the blazing thunder of the automatic ripping and screaming across his low shelter to mash him against the shivering floor. Two deep explosions roared down the hall-way, closing the walls over his head in a shattering rain of gritty dust that stung his eye and filled his mouth with a bitter taste. The automatic fell silent, but the crescendo of gunfire and shouting and stamping boots drowned out any sound from the stairwell. Cautiously, Wager lifted his head above the pile of iron bed rails still hot from the impact of slugs. He felt something dangle on his cheek. The patch. The cloth, still damp from sweat and grimy even in the pale light of the room, hung ripped from his blinking eye, and he tugged it off, feeling the thin glow from the window almost like a cool breeze on his sight.

Suddenly the downstairs clamor died; the gunfire halted as abruptly as it had started. Boots still moved quickly here and there, loud on the bare floors or crackling through broken glass and splinters. There was a murmur of voices and a half-familiar voice said, "Cover me—I'll go see." From outside a voice called, "All right—over here. Line up them sonsofbitches. Over here." And at the foot of the stairs another called out, "Earl, Sheriff Tice is here. He's hurt."

Wager rocked shakily up to his knees and sucked in a lungful of the smoke- and dust-filled air, and he felt the muscles of his neck and shoulders and arms hang like limp cloth from the bones. It was over.

Almost over—there was something else he should remember. An important something else.

But his ears still throbbed from the pummeling concussions, and it was enough right now to kneel here and breathe and not feel the air around him battered into fragments by that automatic.

Then, like a catch in his breath, he remembered. And at the same time he heard a board squeak on the landing.

Groping along the shadowy floor, Wager's fingers found the welcome heft of his pistol. Gingerly, he slid down the wall past the row of beds, ears intent on the cautious sounds in the hallway.

The board creaked again and a tiny scrape told him a hand was feeling its way across the wall toward him. He crouched in the darkest part of the room, trying to get some of the moonglow against the gaping doorway and the black hall beyond. A quiet creak of shoe leather, and the slithering hiss glided to the edge of the doorway and stopped. Perhaps Wager heard shallow breathing in the blackness; perhaps it was his own. He waited, rigid, the weariness fading in the tension of his listening. Slowly, steadily, leather creaked as a vague part of the gloom seemed to congeal and move into the doorway.

"Wager?"

The word was so soft that he wasn't sure he heard it.

"Wager? You there?"

Now things made sense. The pieces of the puzzle that had refused to fit, those unfinished corners and blank spots that he had kept stumbling on, suddenly shifted into place as Wager recognized the voice and knew why the man whispered his name.

"I'm here, Yates."

"Jesus! I thought I'd find you dead." He stepped into the doorway, the glow from the window showing his hands and the pale oval of his face above the dark uniform. A long-barreled shadow was in his right hand. "Where are you?" he asked quietly.

"Over here."

"I can't see . . ." The deputy glided into the room, blurry face intent.

"Stop right there, Yates." Wager clicked the hammer back on his Star PD, and the tiny sound froze the deputy.

"What do you mean, Wager? What the hell are you doing?"

"Seeing things, Yates. Seeing things fall together finally."

"Hey, if you can see in this light—"

"I can see fine. So don't try a thing."

"Try? What are you talking about, man?"

"Mueller's death. And Winston's. Suppose you tell me why you did it, Yates?"

The man's rigid form stood motionless; then he took a step closer and whispered angrily, "Listen, you crazy sonofabitch, I don't know what you're talking about!"

"Somebody wanted Mueller's land, Yates. That's the motive. They wanted his and whoever else's they could scare into selling out. People around here believe in the avenging angels, and by God so do I now. But it wasn't the angels who killed Mueller. It was somebody who could get a copy of that angel drawing. Easy enough to do in the sheriff's office—just reach in the safe, make a copy, and then put back the circular from Pueblo. Then the avenging angels got the blame. The same for Winston. He was killed by somebody who knew he was poking around the courthouse records. By somebody who figured Winston had guessed something when he tried to get in touch with me through the sheriff's office. It wasn't Tice or Earl Hodges. I checked the dispatcher's logs, Yates. When Winston was shot, Earl was chasing a runaway bull east of town, and Tice was in his office. Only you were out of the net—and almost invisible. What's more natural than seeing a sheriff's car cruising the back roads? I haven't looked yet, but I'll bet that when I was shot at, both Tice and Earl can be accounted for; you'll be checked out again. It all adds up, Yates; the lost bullet that killed Mueller—you dug it out of the wall and threw it away and then dug more holes, so you could say you searched for it and couldn't find it. And the use of Carmen Gallegos's name to buy Mueller's place . . . She doesn't exist, does she? All the state cares about is if that name pays taxes. What'd you do, get Mueller drunk and promise to buy his land? Talk him into signing the papers on an IOU? And then shoot him in the back when he wanted his money? That's what those figures on the paper were—principal, interest, payments. You were talking money that you knew you didn't have, and then you shot him."

The standing figure said nothing.

"Then Orrin Winston smelled something. He never really believed the avenging angels killed Mueller. So he poked around the courthouse and you found out about it, didn't you? Went down to Records and bought that old man a cup of coffee and he was happy to tell you who had been looking through what files. When Orrin tried to reach me through the sheriff's office, you really got worried. And when he left work that afternoon, you had a good idea where he was going. So you ambushed him. Maybe he knew it was you who killed Mueller; maybe not. But the safest way for you was an ambush; if he did know you couldn't let him see you. Just like you couldn't chance letting me see you, in case Orrin had said something to Zenas, and Zenas had told it to me. I'll bet you had an avenging angel ready to stick in my hand, too; same clue, same suspects. But the m.o. was different, Yates—the clues were the same but the m.o. was different, and that puzzled me."

He gave the man a chance to reply, but there was only silence.

"And finally Orrin's office—Tice and I scared you off, didn't we? But you naturally came by to do the fingerprint work. Now," Wager said, "you've come up here to make sure I don't get out alive."

From downstairs came the sound of Tice being rolled, groaning, onto a blanket and dragged gently into the kitchen.

"What made Mueller's land so valuable, Yates? I looked at the mineral records for the whole valley—there's nothing there but rock. What in hell was worth killing two men for?"

"Water."

The deputy's voice was flat and weary. "Water for oil-shale development. A million, two million dollars' worth of underground water rights if a man could corner that valley."

And that explained Orrin's final words: it wasn't a plea against thirst, but the clue that had sent him delving into the county records, the clue he had hoped Wager would understand. But Wager had been too dumb.

"All right, Yates." Wager's voice was just as tired. "It's over now. Drop your weapon."

"Why?"

Wager tensed. His eyes watched the dark line that was the barrel of the deputy's .44. "You're covered, Yates." Body armor—Wager remembered that the deputy wore body armor. If the man went for it, Wager would have only a head shot. A snap shot at the head in a dark room. "You won't make it."

"Fuck you!" Yates's weapon fired even as he swung it. The glare and whipping heat slapped at Wager's eyes. He squeezed the trigger and felt the Star buck against his arm, lift, and fall back on target as Yates and he fired second shots together. Wager's own shot was lost in the booming flash of Yates's .44 and the suddenness of a bomb shattered the darkness behind his eyes with a stunning, jolting spray of red and orange that filled his mind as it was plunged into silence.

He did not know how long he was out. The ache drew him from wherever he had gone, pounding heavily between his temples with every heartbeat and spearing the back of his eyeballs. He tried to move, to pull his arm out from under its hot pressure, his legs from wherever they lay in the blackness. But even the thought of moving sent a pulse of pain across his skull and clenched his stomach with nausea. Gradually, beneath the intense focus of the ache, he sensed something different, a feeling more than a sound: the noises had stopped. Almost stopped. The mutter of voices came from somewhere outside his clenched eyelids, and then silence. Wager turned his head gently, the pain slamming like a bowling ball behind his forehead; his cold, probing fingers brushed through the stickily matted hair along his scalp and against the torn, raised flesh where the bullet had creased him. He pressed gingerly around the throbbing soreness, but that's all it was, a crease. On his forearm, a tightly wrapped bandage clamped his skin back together, and he could feel the familiar burn of a cut when he bent his wrist. Slowly, as though tugging weakly at strings, he pulled first one leg and then the other back to his body and tried to sit up. He held the swaying floor as still as possible beneath his spread fingers, but nausea drained his strength and he dropped back with a groan.

"Wager's coming around." The voice was clear but distant, and a moment later he heard the mash of boots on the glass-littered floor.

"Wager? Wager—can you hear me?"

"Uh-huh."

"It's me, Earl Hodges. You know me? You know who I am?"

"I know." Then, "Where's Yates?"

"Dead."

A surge of throbbing closed off his breath for a moment. "He killed Mueller. And Orrin."

"I know some of it. I was coming up the stairs and heard him tell about the water rights. But I couldn't get there in time." Hodges's boot shuffled stickily in some liquid that had seeped over the kitchen floor. "You'll have to write it all out as soon as you're able."

"Tice? How's Tice?"

"He's hurt, but he's a tough old buzzard. We sent him back in the Jeep cussing us all until he passed out. I don't know if he'll make it. I sure hope so."

Wager felt fingers press against his forehead and a thumb at his eyelids. The gesture brought pain jabbing from ear to ear.

"Okay—okay, take it easy. You got a bad concussion and a not-so-bad cut. But I think that's all. An ambulance is on the way, but it'll take a few hours. We'll get you and the others out of here as soon as we can."

"Zenas? His boys?" An undertow of blackness started to pull at him and he had to struggle to hear what Hodges answered.

"He blew hell out of the one with the Thompson sub-machine gun. Then they come down a rope ladder when we broke in. Left you up there alone." Hodges sniffed. "Now he's down the canyon seeing about his people. He said to tell you thanks, but he still thinks they could have done it without any Gentile help. Which is a bunch of crap."

Wager could now squint through half-open eyes. Outside someone had set kerosene lanterns in a circle, and the soft light played over a ring of prisoners who were squatting facing away from each other. Around the circle deputies lounged, rifles on arms, and watched.

"Which one's Willis?"

"That one—the one with the long beard."

He saw only the profile, a thick nose that jutted out over the mustache and gray-streaked beard, a forehead slanting back from bushy eyebrows. The man's back was straight and he stared not at the ground like the others, but levelly and unblinking into the night. The blackness pulled at Wager, a swirling feeling, and gave him time for only that glimpse; but as he slid away, it seemed right that such a vision should be brief.

His room at the county hospital was in the west corridor, and in the afternoons before the nurse came by to turn the blinds against the lowering sun Wager could look across the spray-dotted line of horizon toward a sky whose paleness marked the heat of the benchland. It still took a good deal of effort to overcome the drowsiness that seemed to be a constant state and that made it so difficult to think clearly.

"It will be a few days, Detective Wager, before you feel normal. You're lucky you didn't become comatose. Or worse." The doctor jotted something on the chart, nodded briskly, and went out, a nurse and an orderly in his wake.

After another day or two, he could get up without reeling and could stay awake longer, and he even began to get out of bed and walk the few steps down to Tice's room. He waited until after the midday visiting hours, because the sheriff's wife sat for every minute of every visiting period and held the man's thick fingers, so he and Wager couldn't really talk. In fact, Wager suspected that Tice fell asleep on purpose when his wife's solicitations grew too long.

"Sheriff? You awake?"

"Hell, yes. How come they let you up and keep me in this damn thing?"

"They're afraid your guts will drop out."

"Not after that damn doctor sewed them in so tight. Every goddamn stitch is pulling."

"What did Hodges say about Zenas and his people? They moving out?"

"Naw. They say that's home and that's where they'll stay."

The cost of Willis's raid had been two dogs poisoned, three attackers dead, and three more seriously wounded. The deputies had four wounded, including Tice and Wager, and one dead. But nobody said much about Yates. The surviving attackers, Willis among them, had been trucked off to Denver to face the homicide charges waiting there. That was the place to find out which of them had killed Kruse and the Beauchamps. Besides, the Grant County commissioners said they didn't have funds to feed that many prisoners for the time their trial would take. They were glad to get shut of them.

"Hodges did say," the sheriff went on, "that the Kruse family was out there all right. He thinks Zenas married himself to the widows."

"Sweet Jesus."

"Maybe sweet sixteen by the time he's through."

"Does Zenas think any more of Willis's followers will come up from Mexico?"

"Earl says he's pretty cocky about that. Claims God helped him lead a victory over the Antichrist, and now his Church of God's Peaceful Blessing is shown to be the only true church. Who knows—maybe Zenas will go on the warpath now. I just hope to hell it's in somebody else's county and after I retire."

Back in his own bed, Wager let the ever-present hazy feeling well up and send him to the edge of sleep. He was just about to slide over the rim when the telephone beside his bed buzzed sharply.

"Gabe? How are you?" It was Jo, her voice bright and healthy as usual, and with that special note that seemed to say she was glad to hear him. "Did I wake you?"

"Fine. And no. In fact, I was thinking what a waste all this time in bed is."

"We'll make up for it—I know just the cure."

"That's a fine cure." And it was. "Did Doyle have any luck with the prisoners yet?"

"No. I saw Willis Beauchamp going to the arraignment. He's scary!"

"He won't be scaring anybody for a long time."

"I hope so. But not one of them's admitting anything about the Beauchamp family, not even to their lawyer. The DA indicted them all for the murders and for conspiracy to commit murder. But a lot of them can prove they were in Mexico when the Beauchamp family was killed, and none of the weapons that were found match the ones used in the Beauchamp shootings. It's going to be circumstantial evidence again. Kolagny thinks it's going to be hard to prove."

"Is that bastard the prosecutor?"

"No, the DA himself. I hear he was really angry at Kolagny for taking a reduced plea on the Ellison garroting. Besides," she added, "this case has a lot of publicity— Gargan has a front-page article on it almost every day. And the DA's up for re-election."

Ah, the eccentric wheels of justice. "The ones they don't get for the Beauchamps will be sent up for attempted murder out here."

"They could serve as much time for that as for killing those children. That's ironic."

"Yeah." It wasn't his worry now. He'd done what he could to establish order, and if the law was chaotic that was somebody else's problem. To hell with it.

"Gargan's stories make Sheriff Tice look real good. But he hasn't even mentioned you, Gabe."

"From him, that's a compliment."

"Oh, and Max wanted to know how you feel. Since we

couldn't make Polly's barbecue, he wants to have a little get-together to celebrate your coming back."

Polly. And another get-together. If Wager needed one thing to prove that despite what happened to him the rest of the world went about its own business, it was Polly.

"He really was worried about you, Gabe. He didn't say anything, but you could see it. Gabe? Are you there?"

"I'm here." All he'd have to do was say he didn't feel like it. You say that enough times and people start to leave you alone. Even Polly.

"Max really wanted me to ask you."

Which, of course, was the real issue. "What's she have in mind this time, a luau?"

"It's Max. He wants us all to go to the Brother's. Sandwiches and beer and a big welcome back."

"Oh." Then, "You want to go?"

"Yes!"

So did Wager. "Tell him we'll be there."

After Jo had hung up, Wager lay in the air-conditioned room and drowsily watched the afternoon thunderstorms form where the desert heat of the benchland met the cooler mountain air. The first sign was a wisp, like fraying steam, that lifted swiftly on the thermal drafts. Then the wisp thickened into a pearl-gray haze, and rising out of that came a more defined, thicker cloud that caught the sun whitely on one side while its eastern half was left dark with shadow. Sometimes, farther away, a larger upsweep of cloud towered even higher through gray, windsculpted ledges to fan out into a fluffy mushroom form. Those were the ones that, as they pushed up the mountain flanks, would flatten in the jet stream and shape into anvil heads and sail majestically above the lightning and hail and thundering rains they pounded onto the huddled earth below. Half asleep, he watched one cloud rise and move slowly nearer, towering and twisting silently into a mottled silver-and-black mass, whose center began to look like a standing figure. To each side, billows of inexorably moving cloud fanned and curved and spread like gigantic wings.